The Tobacconist

Robert Seethaler was born in Vienna and divides his time between his home town and Berlin. He is the author of five novels, including the acclaimed *A Whole Life*, which was short-listed for the Man Booker International Prize in 2016.

LEABHARLANN CHONTAE
LIATROMA
LEITRIM COUNTY LIBRARY

Also by Robert Seethaler

A Whole Life

Robert Seethaler

The Tobacconist

Translated by Charlotte Collins

LEABHARLANN CHONTAE
LIATROMA
LEITRIM COUNTY LIBRARY

PICADOR

First published 2016 by House of Anansi Press Inc., Toronto, Canada

First published in the UK 2016 by Picador
an imprint of Pan Macmillan
20 New Wharf Road, London N1 9RR
Associated companies throughout the world
www.panmacmillan.com

ISBN 978-1-5098-0661-4

Copyright © Kein & Aber AG Zürich–Berlin 2012
Translation copyright © Charlotte Collins 2016

The right of Robert Seethaler to be identified as the
author of this work has been asserted by him in accordance
with the Copyright, Designs and Patents Act 1988.

Originally published in 2012 as *Der Trafikant* by Kein & Aber AG Zürich–Berlin.

All rights reserved. No part of this publication may be reproduced,
stored in a retrieval system, or transmitted, in any form, or by any means
(electronic, mechanical, photocopying, recording or otherwise)
without the prior written permission of the publisher.

Pan Macmillan does not have any control over, or any responsibility for,
any author or third-party websites referred to in or on this book.

1 3 5 7 9 8 6 4 2

A CIP catalogue record for this book is available from the British Library.

Printed and bound by CPI Group (UK) Ltd, Croydon, CR0 4YY

This book is sold subject to the condition that it shall not, by way of
trade or otherwise, be lent, hired out, or otherwise circulated without
the publisher's prior consent in any form of binding or cover other than
that in which it is published and without a similar condition including
this condition being imposed on the subsequent purchaser.

Visit **www.picador.com** to read more about all our books
and to buy them. You will also find features, author interviews and
news of any author events, and you can sign up for e-newsletters
so that you're always first to hear about our new releases.

The Tobacconist

One Sunday, in the late summer of 1937, an unusually violent thunderstorm swept over the mountains of the Salzkammergut. Until then, Franz Huchel's life had trickled along fairly uneventfully, but this thunderstorm was to give it a sudden turn that had far-reaching consequences. As soon as he heard the first distant rumble of thunder, Franz ran inside the little fisherman's cottage where he lived with his mother in the village of Nussdorf am Attersee and crawled into bed to listen to the unearthly racket from the safety of his warm and downy cave. The weather shook the hut on every side. The beams groaned, the shutters banged outside, and the wooden roof shingles, thickly overgrown with moss, flapped in the storm. Rain pelted against the windowpanes, driven by gusts of wind, and on the sills a few decapitated geraniums drowned in their tubs. The iron Jesus on the wall above the old clothes box wobbled as if at any moment he might tear himself from his nails and leap down from the cross and from the shore of the nearby lake came the crash of fishing boats slammed against their moorings by the pounding waves.

When the storm finally died down and a first tentative ray of sun quivered towards his bed across soot-blackened floorboards trodden by generations of heavy fishermen's boots, Franz felt a sudden small rush of contentment. He curled up in a ball, then stuck his head out from under the quilt and looked around. The hut was still standing, Jesus still hung on the cross, and through the window, which was sprinkled with drops of water, a single geranium petal shone like a pale red ray of hope.

Franz crawled out of bed and went to the kitchen alcove to boil up a saucepan of coffee and creamy milk. The firewood under the stove had stayed dry, and it flared up like straw. For a while he sat staring into the bright, flickering flames, until the door flew open with a sudden crash. In the low doorframe stood his mother. Frau Huchel was a slender woman in her forties, still quite good-looking, though somewhat gaunt, like most of the local people: work in the surrounding salt mines or cattle sheds or the kitchens of the guesthouses for summer visitors took its toll. She just stood there, panting, one hand resting on the doorpost, head slightly bowed. Her apron stuck to her body; tangled strands of hair hung down over her fore-head, and drops of water were forming and falling one by one from the tip of her nose. Behind her the peak of the Schafberg reared up ominously against the grey, cloud-covered sky, in which blue flecks were already reappearing here and there. Franz was reminded of the lopsided, oddly carved Madonna that someone in the olden days had nailed to the doorframe of the Nussdorf chapel, and which was now weathered almost beyond all recognition.

'Did you get wet, Mama?' he asked, poking about in the

fire with a green twig. His mother raised her head, and then he saw that she was crying. The tears mingled with rainwater, and her shoulders were heaving.

'What's happened?' he asked in alarm, shoving the twig into the smoking fire. His mother didn't answer; instead, she pushed herself off the doorframe and took a few unsteady steps towards him, only to stop again in the middle of the room. For a moment she seemed to look around, as if searching for something; then she raised her hands in a gesture of helplessness and fell forward onto her knees.

Franz stepped forward hesitantly, placed his hand on her head, and started awkwardly stroking her hair.

'What's happened?' he repeated hoarsely. He felt suddenly strange, and stupid. Until now it had been the other way round: he had cried, and his mother had stroked him. Her head felt delicate and fragile under his palm; he could feel the warm pulse beneath her scalp.

'He's drowned,' she said quietly.

'Who?'

'Preininger.'

Franz paused. He rested his hand on her head for a few moments longer, then withdrew it. His mother brushed the strands of hair off her forehead. She stood up, took a corner of her apron and wiped her face with it.

'You're filling the whole cottage with smoke!' she said, pulling the green twig out of the stove and stoking the fire.

Alois Preininger was by his own account the richest man in the Salzkammergut. In fact he was only the third richest; this annoyed him intensely, but it had made him the man he was, notoriously ambitious and pig-headed. He owned a few hectares of forest and pasture, a sawmill, a paper factory, the last four fisheries in the area, an unknown number of plots of land, large and small, around the lake, with the buildings upon them, as well as two ferries, a pleasure steamer, and the only automobile in a radius of more than four kilometres: a magnificent, claret-coloured Steyr-Daimler-Puch. The latter, however, whiled away its time in a rusty tin hut on account of the roads, which were constantly streaming with the incessant rain typical of the Salzkammergut.

Alois Preininger's sixty years didn't show. He was still in the prime of life. He loved himself, his home region, good food, strong drink, and beautiful women — though beauty was subjective, and therefore relative. Essentially, he loved all women, because he found all women beautiful. He had met Franz's mother years earlier at the big lake festival. She was standing beneath the old linden tree wearing a sky-blue dress, and her calves were as light brown, smooth and flawless as the wooden steering wheel of the claret-coloured Steyr-Daimler-Puch. He ordered fresh grilled fish, a jug of cider and a bottle of kirsch, and as they ate and drank they didn't even try not to look at each other. Shortly afterwards they danced the polka, later even waltzes, and whispered little secrets in each other's ears. They walked arm in arm around a lake dotted with stars, found themselves unexpectedly in the tin hut, and then in the back of the Steyr-Daimler-Puch. The back seat was sufficiently broad, the leather soft, the shock absorbers well oiled: all in all, the night was a success. From then on they met frequently in the hut. Their meetings were brief, explosive, and free of all demands or expectations. For Frau Huchel, however, these pleasantly sweaty encounters on the back seat had an additional side effect that was perhaps even slightly more pleasant: punctually at the end of each month a cheque for a not inconsiderable sum of money fluttered into the Nussdorf savings bank. This regular windfall enabled her to move into the former fisherman's cottage right by the lake, to eat a hot meal once a day, and to take the bus to Bad Ischl twice a year and treat herself to a hot chocolate in Café Esplanade and a couple of metres of linen for a new dress from the draper's next door. For her son Franz, on the other hand, the advantage of Alois Preininger's affectionate generosity was that, unlike all the other young lads, he didn't have to spend the whole day crawling around a salt mine or a dung heap somewhere, earning a meagre living. Instead, he could stroll about the forest from dawn till dusk, bare his belly to the sun on one of the wooden jetties, or simply lie in bed when the weather was bad and lose himself in thoughts and dreams. All that was over now, though.

As had been his habit for almost forty years — interrupted only by a very few adverse events, such as the First World War or the big fire at the sawmill — Alois Preininger had spent this Sunday morning at the regulars' table at the Goldener Leopold inn, where he had partaken of roast venison with red cabbage and sliced bread dumplings, as well as eight pints of beer and four glasses of double-distilled schnapps. He had held forth in his deep vibrato bass, making all sorts of important comments about maintaining Upper Austrian customs and traditions, about the Bolshevism that was spreading through Europe like scabies, about the idiotic Jews, the even more idiotic French, and the almost limitless opportunities for development in the tourist industry. At about midday, as he was finally staggering home, rather sleepy, along the path beside the shore, all around him was oddly silent. There were no birds to be seen, no insects to be heard, and even the bluebottles that had buzzed about his sweaty, gleaming neck back at the inn had disappeared. The sky hung heavy over the lake; the surface of the water was completely smooth. Not even the reeds were moving. It was as if the air had congealed and encased the whole landscape in motionless silence. Alois was reminded of the jellied pork at the Goldener Leopold: he should have ordered that, not the roast venison, which was sitting in his stomach like a brick, despite the schnapps. He wiped the sweat from his forehead with his shirtsleeve and gazed out over the expanse of water that extended before him, blue-black and soft as silk. Then he took off his clothes.

The water was pleasantly cool. Alois swam with calm strokes, exhaling into the dark, mysterious depths below him. He had more or less reached the middle of the lake when the first drops fell, and after another fifty metres it was already bucketing down. A steady pattering lay on the surface of the water: hammering drops, thick cords of rain connecting the blackness of the sky to the blackness of the lake. The wind picked up and quickly turned into a storm, whipping the waves into foamy crests. A first flash of lightning momentarily bathed the lake in unreal, silvery light. The thunder was deafening, crashes that seemed to tear the world apart. Alois laughed out loud and thrashed his arms and legs wildly. He shouted with delight. Never had he felt so alive. The water around him was bubbling, the sky above him collapsing, but he was alive. He was alive! He thrust his torso out of the water and crowed up at the clouds. At precisely that moment a bolt of lightning struck his head. An incandescent brightness filled the inside of his skull, and for a fraction of a second he had something like a premonition of eternity. Then his heart stopped, and with an expression of astonishment, and wrapped in a shroud of delicately glistening bubbles, he sank to the bottom of the lake.

The funeral took place in the Nussdorf parish cemetery and was well attended. Many people from the area had come to bid farewell to Alois Preininger. Above all, a conspicuous number of black-veiled women gathered around the grave. There was a great deal of weeping and sobbing, and Horst Zeitlmaier, the longest-serving foreman at the sawmill, placed the three finger stumps of his right hand on his breast and wrung out a few words in a trembling voice. 'Preininger was a good man,' he said. 'As far as we know, he never stole from or cheated anyone. And he loved his home like no other. Even as a small boy he always liked to jump into the lake. Last Sunday it was for the very last time. Now he's with God, and we wish him well. In the name of the Father, the Son and the Holy Ghost, amen!'

'Amen!' replied the others. 'And he still had such an appetite!' someone whispered, and those standing around nodded sorrowfully. A choked sob was heard from beneath one of the black veils, a few words were exchanged here and there; then the crowd dispersed.

On the way home, Franz's mother lifted her veil and blinked, red-eyed, at the sunshine. The lake lay quiet, shimmering dully. In the shallow water a heron stood motionless, waiting for the next fish. On the far shore one of the ferries hooted to announce its departure. The Schafberg stood behind it like a painting, and swallows darted through the clear air.

'Preininger's gone,' she said, placing her hand on Franz's arm, 'and the times aren't getting any better. Something's in the air.' Franz instinctively looked up at the sky, but there was nothing there. His mother sighed. 'You're seventeen already,' she said. 'But you still have such delicate hands. Delicate and soft and white, like a girl's. A boy like you can't work in the forest. Certainly not on the lake. And the summer visitors wouldn't know what to make of you, either.' They had stopped walking; her hand lay light and warm on his arm. The ferry had cast off and began to pound slowly across the lake.

'I've been having a bit of a think, Franzl,' said his mother. 'There's this old friend of mine. He spent a summer splashing around in the lake with us once, many years ago. Otto Trsnyek's his name. And this Otto Trsnyek owns a tobacconist's, right in the heart of Vienna. A proper tobacconist's, with newspapers, cigarettes and all the trimmings. That's already something, and what makes it even better is that he owes me a favour.'

'What for?'

His mother shrugged and plucked at a fold in her veil with her fingertips. 'It was a hot summer that year, and we were young and foolish . . .'

On the shore the heron suddenly lifted its head, stabbed the air twice with its beak, spread its wings and took off. They watched it fly for a while until eventually it descended and vanished behind the line of reeds.

'Don't worry, Franz, this was long before you fell into my lap,' she said. 'Anyway, I wrote to him. Otto Trsnyek. To see if he had any work for you.'

'And?'

Instead of answering, his mother reached into her black knitted jacket and took out an official-looking slip of paper. It was a telegram in neat blue capitals: THE BOY CAN COME STOP BUT DONT EXPECT TOO MUCH STOP THANKS STOP OTTO STOP

'And what does that mean?' asked Franz.

'It means you're off to Vienna tomorrow!'

'Tomorrow? But I can't . . .' he stammered, aghast. A moment later his mother wordlessly slapped his face. The blow caught him so suddenly he staggered sideways.

The next day Franz was sitting in the early train to Vienna. To save money he and his mother had walked the thirteen kilometres to Timelkam station. The train was on time, their leave-taking brief; everything was already said and done, after all. She kissed him on the forehead; he acted a bit grumpy, nodded to her and boarded the train. As the old diesel locomotive picked up speed, Franz craned his head out of the window and saw his waving mother on the platform grow smaller and smaller until she finally disappeared altogether, a faint speck in the summer morning light. He fell back in his seat, closed his eyes and exhaled until he grew slightly dizzy. He had left the Salzkammergut only twice in his life. Once they had gone to Linz to buy a suit for his first day of elementary school, and another time there'd been a class trip to Salzburg where the students had listened to a dreary brass concert and spent the rest of the day stumbling around the ancient walls. But those were merely excursions. 'This is something different,' he said quietly to himself. 'Something completely and utterly different!' In his mind's eye the future appeared like the line of a far distant shore materializing out of the morning fog: still a little blurred and unclear, but promising and beautiful, too. And all of a sudden everything felt somehow light and agreeable. It was as if much of his body weight had remained behind with the hazy figure of his mother on Timelkam Station platform. Now Franz was sitting in the train compartment, almost weightless, feeling the rhythmic juddering of the sleepers beneath his seat and hurtling towards Vienna at the unimaginable speed of eighty kilometres an hour.

An hour and a half later, when the train emerged from the Alpine foothills and the broad, bright, hilly landscape of Lower Austria opened up before him, Franz had already consumed the entire contents of the pack of maternal provisions and felt, once again, as heavy as he always did.

The journey passed without notable incident; in fact, it was rather boring. The train had to make only one unscheduled stop, on the stretch between Amstetten and Böheimkirchen. A violent jolt passed through the carriages and they rapidly lost speed. Items of luggage tumbled down from the nets, there was an ear-splitting screech, cursing and shouting all around, then another jolt, even more violent than the first — and the train came to a halt. The train driver had had to hang his entire body weight from the cast iron brake lever as a large, dark, heaped-up sort of object — a suspicious one, at any rate — had suddenly appeared on the tracks a short way ahead. 'Probably the Socialists again,' growled the ticket inspector as he hurried through the carriages to the front of the train, ticket pad flapping. 'Or the National Socialists! Or whatever — they're all the same riffraff!'

It soon became clear, however, that the suspicious object was just an old cow that had chosen to die on the tracks of the western railway, of all places, and now lay heavy and stinking on the sleepers. With the help of some of the passengers (and closely observed by Franz, who stood at a safe distance with his soft girl's hands clasped behind his back), they managed to drag the cadaver off the tracks. The cow's dark eyes shimmered beneath a mad crawl of flies. Franz was reminded of the glistening stones he had so often collected from the shore of the lake as a boy and carried home in the bulging pockets of his trousers. Every time he shook the trousers out over the cottage floor he had been surprised by a twinge of disappointment as the stones rolled dull and dry across the floorboards, their enigmatic lustre gone.

When the train finally pulled into Vienna West Station, only two hours late, and Franz stepped out of the station concourse into the bright midday light, his little moment of melancholy had long since passed. Instead, he suddenly felt slightly sick and had to hang on to the post of the nearest gas lamp. How embarrassing if the first thing you do is pass out in front of everyone, he thought crossly. Just like the pasty-faced summer visitors: year after year, scores of them would collapse on the grass, stricken with heatstroke, soon after arriving at the lake and would have to be revived by good-humoured locals with a bucket of water or a slap or two. He clung even tighter to the lamppost, closed his eyes and didn't move until he could feel the pavement safe beneath his feet again, and the reddish spots slowly pulsing across his field of vision had dissolved. When he opened his eyes again, he gave a short, startled laugh. It was overwhelming. The city seethed like the vegetable stew on Mother's stove. Everything was in constant motion; even the walls and streets seemed alive, breathing, bulging. It was as if one could hear the groaning of cobblestones and the grinding of bricks. The noise — there was an incessant roaring in the air, an incomprehensible jumble of sounds, tones and rhythms that peeled away, flowed into each other, drowned each other out, shouted, bellowed over each other. And the light. Everywhere a flickering, a sparkling, flashing and shining: windows, mirrors, advertising signs, flagpoles, belt buckles, spectacle lenses. Cars rattled past. A truck. A dragonfly-green motorcycle. Another truck. A tram rounded the corner with a piercing ring of the bell. A shop door was wrenched open, car doors slammed. Someone trilled the first few bars of a popular melody but broke off halfway through the chorus. Someone cursed hoarsely. A woman screeched like a hen being slaughtered. Yes, thought Franz, in a daze: this is something different. Something completely and utterly different. And at that moment he became aware of the stench. Something seemed to be fermenting beneath the pavement, and all sorts of vapours hovered above it. It smelled of sewage, of urine, of

cheap perfume, old fat, burned rubber, diesel, horseshit, cigarette smoke, road tar.

'Are you feeling unwell, young man?' A little lady stood
in front of Franz, looking up at him with red, inflamed eyes.
Despite the midday heat she wore a heavy loden coat, and a
shabby fur hat on her head.

'No, no!' said Franz quickly. 'It's just so noisy in the city.
And it stinks a bit. I suppose it's the canal.'

The little lady pointed her forefinger at him, like a withered twig.

'It's not the canal that stinks,' she said. 'It's the times. Rotten
times, that's what they are. Rotten, corrupt and degenerate!'

On the other side of the street a horse and cart rumbled past, piled high with beer barrels. One of the massive
Pinzgauers arched its tail and let fall a few droppings, which
a scrawny boy, trotting along behind purely for this purpose,
scraped up with his bare hands and stuffed into the sack on
his shoulder.

'Have you come from far away?' asked the little lady.

'From home.'

'That's very far. The best thing you can do is turn around
and go straight back!'

A vein in her left eye had burst and expanded into a rosy
triangle. Tiny clumps of coal dust were stuck to her eyelashes.

'Nonsense!' said Franz. 'There's no going back, and anyway, one can get used to anything.'

He turned and walked off, crossed the ring road in heavy traffic, dodged a speeding omnibus at the very last moment, sprang lightly over a puddle of horse piss and turned into Mariahilferstrasse, the street across from the station, just as his mother had told him. When he looked behind him, the little lady was still standing by the streetlamp at the entrance to the station, a loden-green dwarf with an outsize head and sunlight glowing in the fine tips of her fur hat.

Otto Trsnyek's little tobacconist's shop was in Vienna's ninth district, on Währingerstrasse, squeezed in between Veithammer Installations and the Rosshuber butcher's. A large metal sign above the entrance read:

Trsnyek Tobacconist's
Newspapers
Stationery
Tobacco Products
est. 1919

Franz smoothed his hair with a little saliva, buttoned his shirt right up to the collar, which he felt lent him a certain air of seriousness, took a deep breath and entered the shop. A soft tinkle of little bells sounded from the doorframe above his head. Hardly any light made it into the interior through the posters, leaflets and advertisements that almost completely covered the shop window, and it took a few seconds for Franz's eyes to adjust to the gloom. The store itself was tiny and crammed to the ceiling with newspapers, magazines, notebooks, books, writing utensils, cigarette packets, cigar boxes and various other tobacco products, items of writing equipment and small goods. Behind the low sales counter, between two tall stacks of newspapers, sat an older man. His head was bent over a file, and he was entering figures, carefully and with great concentration, into columns and boxes clearly designated for this purpose. A muffled quiet filled the room; the only sound was the scratch of pen nib on paper. Dust glimmered in the few narrow rays of light, and there was a strong smell of tobacco, paper and printer's ink.

'Hello, Franzl,' said the man, without looking up from his numbers. He said it quietly, but in those cramped surroundings the words were surprisingly clear.

'How do you know who I am?'

'You've still got half the Salzkammergut stuck to your feet!' The man pointed his fountain pen at Franz's shoes, where a few clumps of dark earth clung to the stitching around the toes.

'And you're Otto Trsnyek.'

'Precisely.' With a weary wave of his hand Otto Trsnyek closed his file and slipped it into a drawer. Then he hauled himself out of his little armchair, disappeared behind the pile of newspapers with a peculiar hop, and came straight back out again with two crutches under his armpits. As far as Franz could tell, all that remained of his left leg was half a thigh. The trouser leg was sewn up in a flap that dangled below the stump and swung back and forth slightly with every movement. Otto Trsnyek lifted one of the crutches and with a circular, almost tender gesture indicated the range of products in the store.

'And these are my acquaintances. My friends. My family. If I could, I'd keep them all.' He leaned his crutches against the counter and ran the back of his hand softly over the covers of the colourful, shiny magazines on one of the shelves. 'But still I give them out, every week, every day, at all hours, from opening to closing. And do you know why?'

Franz didn't know.

'Because I'm a tobacconist. Because I want to be a tobacconist. And because I'll always be a tobacconist. Until I can't do it any more. Until the good Lord rolls down my shutters. It's that simple!'

'Aha,' said Franz.

'Precisely,' said Otto Trsnyek. 'And how's your mother?'

'Same as ever, really. She said to send you her regards.'

'Thanks,' said Otto Trsnyek. And then he initiated his apprentice into the secrets of the tobacconist's life.

Franz's main workplace would be the little stool by the front door. He was to sit there quietly (when there was nothing more urgent to do), not talk, wait for instructions, and otherwise work on extending his mind and horizons, which was to say: read newspapers. Because reading newspapers was the only important, the only meaningful and relevant part of being a tobacconist; furthermore, if you didn't read newspapers it meant you weren't a tobacconist, or even that you weren't really human. However, the proper reading of newspapers could not, of course, be understood simply as a quick leaf-through of one or maybe two miserable tabloids. The correct reading of newspapers, equally extending both mind and horizon, encompassed *all* the newspapers on the market (and therefore also in the shop), if not from cover to cover then at least in greater part, meaning: front page, editorial, the most important columns, the most important commentaries, and the most important reports in the sections Politics (Domestic and Foreign), Regional, Economy, Science, Sport, Arts, Society, and so on. It was a well-known fact that the sale of newspapers constituted the core business of every serious tobacconist's, and the customer, or rather the newspaper buyer — insofar as he was not one of the many who, for intellectual or emotional or political reasons, were regular readers of a particular publication — wanted the newsagent to advise and inform him accordingly, and if necessary guide him, with gentle emphasis, or emphatic gentleness, towards the paper that on this day, at this hour, in this mood, was the only appropriate one for him, the customer, the reader, the newspaper buyer. Had Franz understood this properly?

Franz nodded.

Then there were the tobacco products. With cigarettes it

was pretty easy. Any country bumpkin who happened to come along from the Salzkammergut or wherever it might be and accidentally bumbled into a tobacconist's could sell cigarettes. Cigarettes were to a tobacconist what bread rolls were to a baker. Everyone knew that you didn't buy either bread rolls or cigarettes for their taste or the way they looked; the only reason you bought them was because you were hungry or addicted. And with that you'd said and noted pretty much everything you needed to know about the sale of both bread rolls and cigarettes. Cigars, now, were a very different matter — *very* different! Only by selling cigars could a serious tobacconist's become the perfect tobacconist's; only the aroma, the scent, the taste and flavour of a proper range of cigars transformed a standard newspaper kiosk with smoking accessories into a temple of mind and senses. Could Franz follow all that, more or less?

Franz nodded and sat down on his stool.

The problem, said Otto Trsnyek, glancing sadly at the wall rack packed tightly with boxes of cigarettes all the way up to the ceiling — the big problem for the cigar business (and for many other things as well, incidentally) was politics. Politics always messed up absolutely everything, so it didn't really make much difference whose fat bum currently occupied the seat of government — the late Kaiser, the dwarf Dollfuss, his apprentice Schuschnigg or that megalomaniac Hitler across the border — politics messed up, screwed up, fouled up and dumbed down absolutely everything, and basically ruined it one way or another. The cigarette trade, for example. Especially, and above all, the cigarette trade! There were hardly any cigarettes to be had any more these days! Deliveries got held up; they'd become unreliable and unpredictable; the amount of stock varied hugely, with a steady downward trend; the contents of some of the boxes had been sold weeks and months ago: the boxes were just sitting there empty, as decoration, a sort of sad memento of better days!

'That's how it is and no mistake,' said Otto Trsnyek, observing Franz thoughtfully. Then he took his crutches, swung himself back behind the counter with a couple of hops, took his file out of the drawer, stuck the tip of his tongue between his front teeth and went on scratching away at his accounts.

From that day on Franz appeared in Otto Trsnyek's tobacconist's at precisely six a.m. every day. He had been given the little storeroom at the back of the shop as his living-, bath- and bedroom, so the journey to work was pleasantly short. He himself was surprised by how fresh he felt in the mornings; he would leap up from his mattress, put on his clothes, brush his teeth over the metal washbasin, run his wet fingers through his hair and head out front to start work. For the most part he spent the mornings reading the newspapers on his little stool beside the door without too many interruptions. Under Otto Trsnyek's direction he would stack up a pile of fresh morning papers and set about reading them one after the other. To begin with the work was arduous, and as he read he was often so tired he had to pull himself together in order not to topple onto the floor. There had hardly ever been any proper newspapers back home, with the exception of the monthly Nussdorf parish newsletter, which the mayor's wife wrote herself. The only place where there was always a little pile of newspaper was in the privy next to the elder bush behind the cottage, ripped by his mother into handy squares. Franz had from time to time read a headline, a sentence or two, perhaps even half a paragraph before wiping, but had never derived much benefit from this. Back then, world events had slipped through his hands and under his bottom without ever touching his soul. Now, it seemed, this was changing. Although for the first few days he made very slow progress, he soon grew accustomed to the reporting style, which was usually rather stilted with many clumsy, recurring formulations; he even found himself increasingly capable of extracting the meaning from the various different articles. Finally, after a few weeks, he was able to read the newspapers almost fluently; if not from cover to cover, then at least in greater part. And although their different, sometimes even diametrically opposed views and positions thoroughly confused him, he also derived a certain degree of pleasure from his reading. It was an inkling that he could sense rustling among all those printed letters, a little inkling of the possibilities of the world.

Sometimes he would set the papers aside and take a cigar out of one of the many brightly painted wooden boxes. He would turn it in all directions, hold it up against a chink of light from the display window, examine its brittle, leafy skin with the tips of his fingers and, eyes closed, pass it under his nostrils and sniff it. Each brand had its own particular smell, yet they all had this in common: they bore within them the aroma of a world beyond the tobacconist's, Währingerstrasse, the city of Vienna, beyond even this country and the whole wide continent. They smelled of damp black earth, of giant trees mouldering away in silence, of the roars of predators filling the jungle darkness with longing, of the even greater longing in the songs of Negro slaves that rose up from the shimmering heat of the tobacco plantations into the equatorial sky.

'A bad cigar tastes like horseshit,' said Otto Trsnyek, 'a good one like tobacco. A *very* good cigar, on the other hand, tastes like the world!'

He himself, incidentally, was a non-smoker.

Over the first few weeks Franz got to know the clientele. There were a lot of casual customers, harried individuals who came running in, breathlessly panted their requests, ran back out and were seldom or never seen again, but the majority were regulars. Since being granted the tobacconist's shop a year after the end of the war under the compensation law for invalids, Otto Trsnyek had established himself as a permanent fixture in the Alsergrund. None of the locals had known him as a young man. He had simply appeared one day, swinging down

Währingerstrasse on his crutches; he had put up the big metal sign outside the shop and the chimes above the door, sat down behind the sales counter, and been part of the district ever since, like the Votive Church or Veithammer Installations.

'Watch the customers. Make a mental note of their habits and preferences. A tobacconist's memory is his capital!' he told Franz.

Franz did his best. To begin with he found it difficult to match people to their particular habits and desires, but day by day the connections became clearer. Little by little the chaotic, formless mass of customers began to crystallize into individuals with their own peculiarities, until eventually Franz was even able to greet them by name and use the appropriate title — which in Vienna was absolutely essential. There was, for example, Frau Dr. Dr. Heinzl, who would not even have recognized the university building and had certainly never been inside it. Frau Dr. Dr. Heinzl had been married twice, once to a Jewish dentist and later to a lawyer who on their wedding day was already as old as the hills. Both gentlemen followed the majority of Viennese in making their final journey to the Central Cemetery: their doctorates and titles, however, remained, and were proudly borne thereafter by the widow Heinzl. She wore a bluish wig, fanned her face constantly — even in winter — with a pair of salmon-coloured silk gloves, and ordered a copy of the *Wiener Zeitung* and the *Reichspost* every day in a slightly nasal, aristocratic tone of voice. However, the first customer of the day was the retired parliamentary usher, Kommerzialrat Ruskovetz. Herr Ruskovetz came every morning just after opening time, accompanied by his incontinent dachshund, and asked for the *Wiener Journal* and a packet of Gloriettes. Sometimes he and the tobacconist exchanged a few words about the lousy weather or the idiotic government, while the dachshund left yellowish drops on the floorboards. It was Franz's responsibility to wipe them up afterwards with a damp rag. In the mornings the labourers came crashing in, picked up the *Volksblatt* or the *Kleine Blatt* and asked to buy loose cigarettes, which Otto Trsnyek fished out of a preserving glass and counted into their callused hands. Although some of them already smelled of beer first thing, and they brought in quite a lot of muck from outside on their clumpy shoes, Franz liked the labourers. They didn't talk much, had angular faces, and were generally like the dusty brothers of the forestry workers back home. Then, around midday, the pensioners and students came. The pensioners asked for the Österreichische Woche, the students bought a couple of Egyptian cigarettes, plus the *Wiener Zeitung*, writing paper, and the latest satirical magazines. Old Herr Löwenstein appeared in the early afternoon for one or two packets of Gloriettes. After that it was housewife time. The housewives smelled either of cleaning fluid or cherry liqueur; they talked a lot and asked a lot of questions, and in between they requested the *Kleiner Frauenblatt* or other magazines of interest to the modern woman. Herr Kollerer, a very short-sighted justice department official, dropped in and bought his daily Long Heinrich, a thin, long-stemmed cigarillo, as well as one copy each of the *Bauernbündler* and the *Wienerwald-Bote*. At irregular intervals Red Egon came into the shop. Red Egon was an alcoholic, well-known in the neighbourhood, and — although the party was banned — a Social Democrat who publicly declared his allegiance at every opportunity and at the top of his voice. He was a gaunt figure with a glowering expression, but somewhere behind his high forehead there burned a fire that never seemed to cool. Scarcely had he pushed open the door than he began talking of revolutions, uprisings, upheavals, takeovers that were already well underway somewhere: they would smash this capitalist society, which was built on mountains of the pulverized bones of the worn-down, broken-down, ground-down working classes and thoroughly deserved its downfall. After this he usually stared gloomily at the shelves for a while, eventually decided on a pack of filterless, paid and left. Schoolchildren would tumble in, asking for coloured pencils or the little cards they collected; old ladies wanted to chat; old men wanted peace and quiet, and to look at the magazine covers in silence. Sometimes one of the male customers would ask, in a hoarse voice, if he could take a look in 'the drawer'. This was a certain inconspicuous drawer located under the sales counter that Otto Trsnyek was always careful to keep locked, and which was only ever opened at a customer's specific request. The drawer contained so-called 'erotic magazines' (which the tobacconist referred to as 'wank mags' or 'stroke books' when talking to Franz); they had been strictly forbidden for years. The men would leaf through them for a while, trying to maintain as uninterested an expression as possible; they might then take away one or two pamphlets, which Franz would wrap in brown paper to safeguard them from prying eyes.

'A good tobacconist doesn't just sell tobacco and paper,' said Otto Trsnyek, scratching his stump with the top of his fountain pen. 'A good tobacconist sells enjoyment and pleasure — and sometimes the pleasures are guilty ones!'

One card a week, no more and no less, that was the agreement. 'Franzl,' his mother had said the night before his departure, gently stroking his cheek with the back of her forefinger, 'send me a postcard every week, won't you, because a mother needs to know how her child is doing!'

'All right,' Franz had said.

'But they have to be proper picture postcards. The kind with the pretty photos on them. I'll use them to paper over the patch of mould above the bed, and whenever I look at them I'll always be able to imagine where you are!'

In a corner next to the window display there was a small rack with a colourful selection of greetings cards and picture postcards stacked one above the other. Every Friday after-noon Franz would stand in front of it and select one. Most of them showed one of the famous sights of Vienna: St Stephen's Cathedral in the rosy morning light, the Giant Ferris Wheel under the stars, the opera house, splendidly illuminated, and so on. He almost always opted for a card with a picture that included a park or flowerbed, or at the very least flowerboxes outside the windows of houses. Perhaps the greenery and colours might cheer his mother up a bit in hours of rainy solitude, he thought. Besides, they went better with the patch of mould. He wrote a few lines, and his mother wrote a few lines, and each of them would actually have preferred to speak to the other, or at least to sit quietly beside them listening to the reeds. *My dear Franzl, how are you, dear Mother, well, thank you, the weather's good here, the weather's good here too actually, there's lots to see in the city, there isn't in Nussdorf but that's all right, I'm enjoying the work, the moss needs scraping off the cottage again, with love from your Mama, love from me too, your Franz.* They were calls from home to foreign parts and back again, like the brief touch of a hand, fleeting and warm. Franz put his mother's cards in the drawer of his nightstand and watched the pile grow week by week, lots of little shining Attersees. Sometimes, on quiet evenings, just before he fell asleep, he would hear the lake gurgling softly in the drawer. But that may have been his imagination.

At the beginning of October the first autumn wind blew the heat from the streets and the hats off the heads of passers-by.

From time to time Franz would see a hat roll past the shop, immediately followed by its owner, stumbling along after it. The weather had turned cool, Otto Trsnyek had already indicated that he might light the coal stove again soon, and Franz had started wearing a slightly misshapen brown woollen waistcoat that his mother had knitted for him years ago during long winter hours, snowed in, by the light of the fire in the oven. Despite the confusing developments, and the even more confusing political outlook, business was good. 'People are mad about this Hitler, and about bad news — which is basically one and the same thing,' said Otto Trsnyek. 'It's good for selling papers, anyway — and whatever happens people will always smoke!'

One grey, overcast Monday morning, the chimes rang tentatively and an old man entered the shop. He was not especially tall, and quite slight, even spindly. Although his hat and suit both sat impeccably, they looked like relics from some bygone age. His right hand, crisscrossed by a network of bluish veins, was clenched around the knob of a walking stick, while the left was briefly raised in cursory greeting before vanishing again into one of his jacket pockets. His back was slightly bent; his head craned forward. His white beard was neatly trimmed, and he wore round, black-framed spectacles; behind the lenses his shining brown eyes darted about, perpetually vigilant. But the really unusual thing about the old man's appearance was the effect it had on Otto Trsnyek. As soon as he entered the shop the tobacconist stood up and attempted to hold himself as erect as possible, without crutches, propping one hand on the counter. A single, brief, sideways glance had prompted Franz to leap to his feet as well, so now they were both standing stiffly, like a formal reception committee for this spindly old man.

'Good morning, Professor!' said Otto Trsnyek, discreetly dragging his leg into position. 'Virginias, as usual?'

In the course of his apprenticeship to date, if there was one thing Franz had internalized it was that in Vienna there were as many so-called professors as there were pebbles on the banks of the Danube. In some neighbourhoods even the horse-meat butcher and the brewer's drayman addressed each other as 'Professor'. This time, though, something was different. The tobacconist's way of greeting this man immediately made it clear to Franz that this was a real professor, a proper, genuine one, one who didn't need to swing his title before him like a cowbell to receive the professorial recognition that was his due.

'Yes,' said the old man, with a brief nod, taking off his hat and placing it deliberately in front of him on the counter. 'Twenty. And the *Neue Freie Presse*, please.'

He spoke slowly and so quietly it was hard to understand him. In doing so, he barely opened his mouth. It was as if he managed only by dint of considerable effort to squeeze each individual word out through his teeth.

'Of course, Professor!' said Otto Trsnyek, nodding to his apprentice. Franz took a packet of twenty Virginias and the newspaper from the shelves and placed them on the counter in order to wrap them in brown paper. He felt the old man's gaze upon him; he seemed to be following his every movement with close attention.

'This, by the way, is Franzl,' explained Otto Trsnyek. 'He's from the Salzkammergut and still has a lot to learn.'

The old man craned his neck a little further forward. Out of the corner of his eye Franz could see the folds of skin, thin as crepe paper, spilling over the edge of his shirt collar.

'The Salzkammergut,' he said, with a peculiar contortion of the mouth probably meant to indicate a smile. 'Very nice.'

'From the Attersee!' nodded Franz. And for some reason, for the first time in his life, he was proud of that funny, soggy little part of the world he called home.

'Very nice,' the professor repeated. Then he put a few coins on the counter, tucked the packaged items under his arm and turned to leave. In a single bound Franz was there to open the door. The old man nodded to him and stepped out onto the street, where the wind immediately plucked his beard in all directions. He smells strange, this old man, thought Franz: of soap, onions, cigars, and somehow also, interestingly, of sawdust.

'Who was that, then?' he asked, when he had pushed the door shut. He almost had to force himself to straighten up and relinquish the slightly stooping posture he had adopted without realizing.

'That was Professor Sigmund Freud,' said Otto Trsnyek, allowing himself to fall back into his armchair.

'The idiot doctor?' Franz blurted out, his voice betraying mild alarm. Of course he had already heard of Sigmund Freud. By now the professor's reputation extended not only to the farthest corners of the earth but had even reached the Salzkammergut, where it had stimulated the locals' usually rather dull imaginations. There was talk of all manner of sinister urges, of crude jokes, female patients howling like wolves, and private consultations in which revelations got out of hand.

'That's the one,' answered Otto Trsnyek. 'But he can do a lot more than fix rich idiots' heads.'

'Like what?'

'Apparently he can teach people how to live a decent life. Not everyone, of course; only those who can afford his fees. They say an hour in his consulting room costs as much as half an allotment. But that might be a slight exaggeration. At any rate, he treats people without touching them the way other doctors do. Although . . . he does touch them in a way. Just not with his hands.'

'What else would he touch them with?'

'How should I know!' Otto Trsnyek was starting to get impatient. 'With thoughts or the mind or some such nonsense. It seems to work, anyway, and that's the main thing. So — read your newspapers now and leave me in peace.'

He bent low over a pile of paper he had pulled out of the drawer and, using his fountain pen and a long wooden ruler, began to score it with straight lines.

Franz leaned his forehead against the shop window and peered out through a narrow chink of light. The professor was over there, walking down Währingerstrasse with his parcel under his arm. He was walking slowly, head slightly bowed, taking small, careful steps.

'He actually seems very agreeable, the professor,' said Franz thoughtfully. Otto Trsnyek sighed and raised his eyes again from the depths of his line-drawing.

'He may seem agreeable at first glance, but if you ask me he's a pretty dry old stick in spite of all that brain doctoring. He also has a not inconsiderable problem.'

'What kind of problem?'

'He's a Jew.'

'Aha,' said Franz. 'And why's that a problem?'

'That remains to be seen,' replied Otto Trsnyek. 'We'll find out soon enough!'

For a while his gaze wandered absent-mindedly around the shop as if looking for a safe place to linger. Then he paused and smiled briefly to himself. Finally he bent over his work again. With the corner of a little sponge he carefully tried to dab away an ink blot that had spread between the lines.

Franz was still looking out of the shop window. He'd never really understood this business with the Jews. The newspapers didn't have a good word to say about them, and in the photographs and cartoons they looked either funny or crafty, usually both at once. At least there were some in the city, thought

Franz, real flesh-and-blood Jews, with Jewish names, Jewish hats and Jewish noses. Back home in Nussdorf there wasn't a single one. There, they were, at the very most, terrible or nasty or brainless figures of legend — definitely bad, anyway — that haunted people's imaginations. Down the road the professor was just turning onto Berggasse. A gust of wind caught his hair and puffed it into a feather-light crest that floated above his head for a few seconds.

'The hat! What's he done with his hat?' cried Franz, startled. His eyes fell on the sales counter, where the professor's grey hat was still lying. He leaped forward, picked up the hat and ran out with it onto the street.

'Stop, sir, wait, if I may!' he shouted. Arms flailing, he skidded round the corner onto Berggasse, where in just a few steps he caught up with the professor and breathlessly held the hat out towards him. Sigmund Freud contemplated his somewhat battered headgear for a moment before taking it and drawing his wallet from his jacket pocket in response.

'No, please, Professor, of course — it was nothing!' Franz assured him, with a dismissive sweep of the hand that, even as he was making it, felt slightly too expansive.

'Nothing is a matter of course these days,' said Freud, making a deep dent in the brim of the hat with his thumb. As before, he barely moved his jaw when he spoke; his voice was quiet and strained. Franz had to bend forward a little to be sure to understand absolutely everything. Under no circumstances did he want to miss so much as a single word of the famous man's utterances.

'May I be of assistance?' he asked, and although Freud did his best, he couldn't pull away fast enough to stop Franz from sliding the parcel and the newspaper out from under his arm and pressing them decisively to his chest.

'If you wish,' he murmured. He put his hat on his head and walked off. At first, as he walked with the professor down the steep Berggasse, Franz had a rather odd sensation in his stomach, as if some heavy weight were trying to remind him of the significance of this moment. But after just a few steps the odd, heavy feeling in his stomach disappeared, and as they passed Frau Grindlberger's fragrant Anker bakery he saw himself mirrored in the floury shop window, marching tall and erect with the parcel under his arm and the warm, reflected glow of the professor's fame shining upon him, and suddenly felt very proud and buoyant.

'May I ask you a question, Professor?'

'It depends on the question.'

'Is it true that you can fix people's heads? And afterwards teach them how to live a decent life?'

Freud took off his hat again, carefully pushed a thin, snow-white strand of hair behind his ear, put the hat back on and gave Franz a sideways look.

'Is that what they say in the tobacconist's, or back home in the Salzkammergut?'

'Don't know,' said Franz, shrugging.

'We don't fix anything. But at least we don't break anything, either, which is not at all to be taken for granted in doctors' surgeries these days. We can explain certain aberrations, and in some inspired moments we can even influence the thing we've just explained. That is all,' said Freud through gritted teeth, and it sounded as if every single word was causing him pain. 'But we can't even be certain of that,' he added, with a little sigh.

'And how do you go about it all?'

'People lie down on my couch and start talking.'

'That sounds comfortable.'

'The truth is seldom comfortable,' Freud contradicted him, coughing slightly into the dark blue cloth handkerchief he had pulled from his trouser pocket.

'Hmm,' said Franz. 'I have to think about that.' He stopped, glanced up to one side and tried to collect his thoughts, which were leaping about madly somewhere high above the roofs of the town and well beyond the powers of his own imagination.

'Well?' asked the professor, once the peculiar, rather importunate tobacconist's boy had caught up with him again. 'What conclusion did you reach?'

'None at all for the moment. But that doesn't matter. I'll take time to think about it some more. And I'll buy your books and read them — all of them, from cover to cover.'

Freud sighed again. In fact, he really could not recall ever having sighed so often in such a short space of time.

'Don't you have anything better to do than read old men's dusty tomes?' he asked.

'Like what, Professor?'

'You're asking me? You're young. Get out in the fresh air. Go on a trip. Enjoy yourself. Find yourself a girl.'

Franz stared at him, wide-eyed. A shudder ran all the way through his body. Yes, he thought, yes, yes, yes! A moment later it burst out of him: 'A girl!' he cried, so piercingly that the three old ladies who had huddled together on the other side of the street for a quick gossip turned their artfully marcelled heads towards them in alarm. 'Yes, if only it were that simple.'

At last he had voiced the thing that had been agitating both his brain and his heart for some time now, basically since the day his first pubic hairs tentatively began to sprout.

'The vast majority of people have managed it up till now,' said Freud, using his cane with great precision to nudge a pebble off the pavement.

'But that doesn't mean I'll manage!'

'And why wouldn't you, of all people?'

'Where I come from, people might understand a bit about the timber industry and how to get summer visitors to part with their money. They don't understand the first thing about love.'

'That's not unusual. Nobody understands anything about love.'

'Not even you?'

'Especially not me!'

'But why is everybody always falling in love all over the place, then?'

Freud stopped. 'Young man,' he said, 'you don't have to understand water in order to jump in head first.'

'Oh!' said Franz, for want of more suitable words capable of expressing the fathomless depth of his unhappiness. And again, immediately afterwards: 'Oh!'

'Be that as it may,' said Freud, 'we've arrived. May I have my cigars and my newspaper back?'

'But of course, Professor!' said Franz, hanging his head. He handed him the parcel. The little plaque above the entrance to the building read BERGGASSE No. 19. Freud fumbled for and extracted a bunch of keys, unlocked the heavy wooden door and leaned his slight body against it.

'May I . . .'

'No, you may not,' growled the professor, hurriedly squeezing through the crack in the door. 'And remember,' he added, sticking his head out again. 'With women, it's like with cigars: if you pull at them too hard, they won't give you any pleasure. I wish you a good day!'

With that he disappeared into the darkness of the hallway. The door closed with a gentle creak, and Franz stood alone in the wind.

Postcard of the city park full of spring blossom, in the foreground a horse-drawn carriage festooned with lilac.

Dear Mother,

Guess who I met yesterday — Herr Professor Dr. Sigmund Freud! Did you know he's a Jew? And lives right around the corner from the tobacconist's? I walked with him, and we talked for a bit. Very interesting! I think we'll see each other quite often now. How are you? I am well.

Your Franz

Postcard of the Attersee with swans, bathed in golden morning light.

My dear Franzl,

That story about Professor Freud was nonsense, wasn't it? If it isn't nonsense, though, please ask him whether all the things we hear are true. About the urges and all the other stuff. Actually no, it's better you don't ask, who knows what sort of impression that would make. I didn't know he was a Jew. That might not be pleasant, but we'll just have to wait and see. We've had snow here already. Today I'm going into the forest to cut myself a basket of wood. With love,

Your Mama

The professor's words had burned themselves deep into Franz's soul. Especially the ones about girls. *The majority of people have managed it up till now*, he had said. And, contrary to all Franz's doubts in this regard, this hadn't sounded bad at all, but somehow optimistic and irrefutable. Overall, the professorial presence had a rocklike steadfastness about it, despite the brittle frailty of old age. All right, thought Franz, if that's how it is, I'll just have to do something about it.

And so the following Saturday, shortly before the tobacconist's released him for the weekend with a final, encouraging jingle of the bells, he donned his Sunday suit, washed his face, neck and hands with an expensive bar of curd soap bought especially for the occasion, greased his hair with a lump of lard and rubbed his armpits with the petals of a few magnificent roses, plucked in a nocturnal foray to the meticulously planted flowerbeds around the Votive Church. Then, shining and scented, he stepped out onto the street, where the mild autumn light had warmed the cobbles, and took the tram to the Viennese Prater to seek his fortune in the shape of a suitable girl.

The Giant Ferris Wheel was visible from afar, but only when he was standing right underneath it was he fully able to appreciate the dimensions of this remarkable steel monster. The Giant Ferris Wheel wasn't just big; it was gigantic. The clouds seemed to hang barely higher than the highest steel girder. The passengers in the topmost cabins were as small as insects, their arms and scarves barely discernible beyond a tiny wave or flutter.

At the Eisener Mann pub he bought himself a glass of beer. The beer was cold and crisp, and when he blew on it gently the foam flew up in little snow-white clouds. There wasn't a single woman in the bar, apart from an ageing waitress with sad, deep-set eyes. So he paid and headed off to the Mirror Maze.

He wandered around its glassy corridors for quite some time without finding the exit, until at last a man in short trousers showed him the way out. Then he stood for a while in front of the aeroplane carousel, watching the planes zooming round in circles, until he started to get dizzy and went over to the Walfisch tavern, where he sat in the garden and ordered himself a glass of black coffee with whipped cream. The coffee was very black, and the cream tasted almost as sweet as it did in the Café Esplanade in Bad Ischl. The tall chestnut trees rustled quietly, the sun flashed through the leaves, and sparrows hopped about on the gravel. The people sitting at the tables seemed to have had lots of fun already: friendly, open faces all around. A confusion of voices had spread over the garden like an invisible flock of birds, with a solitary, bright laugh fluttering up from time to time. All this merriment made Franz feel rather bitter. He paid and went over to the pony carousel. The beasts were trotting round in circles, heads hanging, carrying children on their backs. A man with an enormous camera was taking pictures to sell to the parents later. There was a lot of laughing, hugging and kissing. The young mothers were almost more beautiful than their children; the young fathers stood proud and erect and gave the attendants tips. One of the ponies raised its tail with a snort and some droppings plopped into the sand. Its eyes reflected the blue autumn sky and, beyond it, the inkling of a freedom that contained neither children's bottoms nor carousels. At the stall next door Franz bought

two Hungarian meatballs dripping with fat, and, to cancel out
the strong garlicky taste, an enormous stick of pink candyfloss.
Immediately afterwards he was overcome with nausea, which
he washed down with another mug of beer, then he went over
to the Grotto Train, where he was the only adult to squeeze
himself into one of the little blue wagons. Juddering slightly,
the ride passed through fantastical landscapes blanketed in a
thick layer of dust. Fairytale characters were standing, sitting,
walking all around. Little Red Riding Hood trudged through
the wood, the Frog Prince squatted on the edge of the well,
Rumpelstiltskin leaped round the fire, and right behind him
Rapunzel let down her flaxen hair from the window of the
tower. Franz thought of home. Years ago, his mother had read
these stories to him from a well-thumbed book. At the time he
was so small that he could comfortably curl up in her lap and
listen to the words falling down on him like soft, warm drops.
As Franz was jolting slowly past Cinderella the first tears came,
and by the time the ride circled the gingerbread house he was
already sobbing into his hands. Hot waves welled up inside him
one after another and shook him from head to foot. He thought
of the cottage, the stove, the lake, his mother, and beyond the
thick veil of his tears the fairytale landscape slid past in a single
blurred stream of colour.

When the young fairground attendant leaning with sleepy
nonchalance against the exit saw Franz come juddering out of
the gloomy grotto into the bright sunlight, doubled up and with

tears streaming down his face, he flicked away his roll-up in a wide arc and summoned the fullness of his capacity for sensitive consolation: 'Life ain't no fairy tale, mate — but never mind, it'll all be over anyway, one of these days!'

Outside, Franz wiped his face with his sleeve a few times and blew his nose into the handkerchief, which in fact he had only brought for the purpose of wiping the chair or hot brow or whatever of some girl who might chance to appear. Slowly he walked on past the rides, past shooting galleries and food stalls, past the dodgems, past the Watschenmann punchbag, past Big Bertha the high striker, past the colourful Ferris wheel, past the Big Ghost Train. Somewhere deep inside him he felt another quiet splash, a last little wave of sadness; then it was over.

But just after he had taken the firm decision to sink the rest of the afternoon in large quantities of beer and other drinks and was about to enter the shady beer garden of the Stiller Zecher, another, far bigger, hotter, wilder wave seized him, washed over him and shook him to the core. Directly in front of him, perhaps ten metres away, a face rose up into the sky: a girl's round face, bright and laughing, framed by a halo of straw-blonde hair. It was the most beautiful face Franz had ever seen (and that included the many brightly painted cover-girl faces in Otto Trsnyek's stock of magazines). High above him, dizzyingly high, this face hung there for a moment, a rosy dot in the blue expanse of the sky, let out a shriek of delight, then immediately swooped down, hair flying, only to rise again a second later. This second was precisely what it took for Franz to grasp that he was standing in front of a swing. An enormous swing whose boats were pitching up and down like ships on the high sea. A wooden sign above the entrance announced, in sweeping brushwork: THE MIGHTY ASSAULT BOAT! HIGHLY AMUSING! FOR ALL AGES! EVERYBODY HAS FUN! EVERYBODY LAUGHS! PLEASE COME ABOARD! Franz decided he would not move. Motionless, eyes still glued to the girl's face as it swooped up and down, he waited until the boats had stopped swinging and the passengers came stumbling out, laughing and squealing. When the girl (flanked by two female friends, though he was aware of these only as formless, faceless, insignificant shadows) finally came walking towards him, he mustered all his strength to wrench himself out of his self-imposed rigidity, clenched his fists in his trouser pockets and stood in her path with a decisiveness that flared up suddenly from the unexplored depths of his soul, lending his words — or so it seemed to him at that moment — an almost luminous emphasis. 'Good afternoon, my name is Franz Huchel, I'm originally from the Salzkammergut and I would like to ride the Ferris wheel with you!'

Interestingly, the girl did not laugh along with her friends, but observed him for a while, like a visitor at the zoo observing an animal of an almost-extinct species. Finally she rested her gaze on his flickering eyes, from which the resolve had long since faded, and said, 'Ferris wheel no, but can we go shooting, please?'

To be precise, she didn't say 'can we go shooting' but 'ken vee go shootink'. There was a discernible flattening of the vowels common among the many people of Bohemian origin who lived in Vienna. A Bohemian girl, then, thought Franz, though he was unable to derive anything useful from the thought. He wordlessly offered her his arm to escort her to the big shooting gallery. Happily, her two friends said good-bye immediately, and swiftly attached themselves to the broad shoulders — decorated with an impressive array of medals — of two rather merry Austrian army officers.

At the shooting gallery a balding man with a scarred head and vacant expression explained the rules. You could choose whether to aim at targets, balloons or colourful Turks' heads. If you shot a hole in a Turk's face you got a few extra points; if you hit a specific spot on his forehead his turban clapped open, tipping forwards with a dull wooden sound, and you got a free round. You could win candy canes, paper roses, or a bunch of real lavender. Out of the corner of his eye Franz saw the Bohemian girl lean forwards, put the rifle to her cheek and curl her finger over the trigger. The finger was short, rosy and round. In fact, everything about her was round: the little ears, the nose, the domed forehead, the arched eyebrows, the big, brown eyes. Her gaze was levelled calmly at the black centre of the target. He would have liked to immerse himself in that gaze, those eyes, to dive head first into bliss. He was reminded of the wooden rain barrel at home, right beside the entrance to the cottage. The water in it was different to the water in the lake. It was brownish and cloudy and smelled a bit funny. The young Franz had once been unable to resist it any longer — out of curiosity, and because it was so hot, in mid-August, at the end of the summer holidays. He had carefully flicked every one of the thin-legged water striders off the surface of the water, taken three deep breaths, and finally plunged his head and half his upper body into the barrel. Inside, it was pleasantly cool. Tiny particles were suspended in the water like dark snow, and the bottom was covered in a thick layer of leaves that had already half turned to mould. He stretched out his arms and stirred up the leaf mass with his fingers. It felt horrible. Slimy and cold, but also nice, in a way. He shuddered as his fingertips encountered something soft, plump and hairy. The body of a dead rat materialized through the thick veil of floating parti-cles. It must have slipped into the barrel fairly recently, and hadn't been able to climb back up the mossy wall by itself. It was lying on its side, its body almost entirely preserved except for a deep, black, gaping hole where the left eye should have been. Franz began to scream, and the rat disappeared behind the fat bubbles of his breath. He surfaced, scrambled out of the barrel and started running. Still screaming, he ran around the house, across the meadow and down to the shore, where his mother was hanging large pieces of linen on the line between two birch trees. He crept under her skirt, clasped her knees and knew that he would stay down there for the rest of his life, or at least until the end of the summer holidays, sitting in safety between his mother's slender thighs.

He heard a *plop* as she fired and hit the mark. She did a little skip on the tips of her toes and squealed with delight, but immediately brought the gun back into position. Franz tried to swallow away the dryness in his mouth. He had just noticed the tip of her tongue between her front teeth: a little pink animal that ventured cautiously out into the open, briefly, damply, touched the upper lip before darting back into its cave, then promptly reappeared, feeling its way around the row of teeth that shimmered like a string of pearls, interrupted by a dark gap in the middle. Never would he have believed it possible that one day the gap between a pair of Bohemian teeth would stir him like this. Juices were surging so violently around his body that for a moment he feared he would lose his inner stability and collapse at her feet like an empty sack. There was another *plop*, and one of the Turks lost his turban. 'Boom, dead!' the girl cried, and Franz could only look on helplessly as her upper lip puckered ever so slightly. With a gentle nudge of her hips she prompted him to take aim. He obeyed, but his hands were shaking; furthermore, he was bothered by a painful erection that he was trying to hide by pressing his loins as close as possible to the planks of the shooting gallery. He too made a *plop*, but the shot went wide. The girl laughed, the shooting gallery attendant laughed, and even the Turks' heads seemed to be baring their golden teeth on his account. Although the sun had now disappeared behind the tops of the fairground rides, he was sweating. The sweat ran down his back in a thin rivulet and gathered in the waistband of his underpants. He squeezed an eye shut and fired again. *Plop*. Missed. He would have liked to run away, far away, to his room at the back of the shop, home to his bed beside the lake, or just back to the grotto train to circle the dusty fairy-tale gloom in solitude for the rest of his days. Then, suddenly, he felt her hand on his behind. She had put down the gun and was smiling at him. 'You no can shoot, but you got nice ass!' she said, and at that moment he realized he was lost.

They went over to the Schweizerhaus, where a band was playing in the pub's spacious garden and colourful Chinese lanterns glimmered at the tops of the trees. They ordered two mugs of Budweiser from a moustachioed waiter, and two potato fritters that crackled gently as they bit into them. The hot fat squirted out and dripped onto the tablecloths. The girl spoke to the waiter in Czech, and as Franz listened to the strangely dark intonation of their language he contemplated the puckering of her upper lip with the absent expression of a man in a dream. She laughed, and the moustache laughed, and before Franz could send him away to fetch another two beers she leaned across the table towards him, put her hand on his cheek and kissed him in the middle of his forehead. 'We dance now!' she cried, and Franz's face lit up like the lanterns in the chestnut tree above him.

Arm in arm they passed through the rows of tables to the dance floor, and when they felt the rhythmic quaking of the boards beneath their feet she turned to him, put one hand on his shoulder, circled his waist with the other, and started to sway in time to the music. Franz couldn't dance, and didn't like to do so. At home he had always declined to shuffle around in circles with the plump country girls, their breasts almost bursting out of their dirndls, grinning up at him out of shiny moon faces. He'd always avoided the Sunday morning gatherings at the Goldener Leopold, too; even at the lake festival in summer he'd always sat on the sidelines, motionless and silent, lost in thoughts that flew far out over the surface of the water. But now he was dancing. At first his movements were a little stiff and hesitant, but soon they became softer, smoother and freer, until at last, in a moment of blessed mindlessness, he let himself go, let himself fall into the arms of this round Bohemian queen, let himself drift and be rocked and swayed by her. He felt her hand wander slowly round his hip and land on his behind again. He looked into her eyes, saw her smile, saw that slight puckering of her upper lip, saw the gap between her teeth. And when he felt her bosom pressed against his belly he finally abandoned all attempts to hide his erection, which by now had swelled to monstrous proportions.

They danced until their feet were burning. Each song was a little more sentimental and a little more heartrending than the last: 'You're My Lucky Star,' 'Merci Mon Ami,' 'I'll Dream

Of You Every Night,' 'Paris, You're The Most Beautiful City In The World,' 'My Heart Only Ever Cries Out For You,' 'O Marita,' and so on. After about the tenth song the musicians, needing a beer break, left the stage and headed for the bar. The girl was still glued to Franz's overheated body, and all of a sudden he felt her lips on his ear. 'Have drunk, have danced — what we do now?' she whispered, and Franz didn't need a mirror to know that he was smiling like a blissful idiot and his face was as red as a beetroot.

'I still have two and a half schillings,' he said, his voice cracking slightly. 'That's either four mugs of beer, a couple of rounds at the shooting gallery, or two turns on the Ferris wheel!'

The girl stepped back and looked at him. It was a look of incredulous astonishment, and for the briefest of moments it seemed to Franz that her warm brown eyes had hardened. Like amber, he thought — like the two drops of amber he had seen once in first grade, in the local history exhibition in Bad Ischl, but darker and bigger and with no insect embedded in them. A second later, though, her eyes were shining again; her features relaxed, and she started to laugh. It was short laughter, high and sharp, like her shriek of delight at the top of the swingboat. She gave Franz a hug and a smacking kiss on the cheek. 'Back soon, sonny boy!' she said, turned, and walked off. Mesmerized, Franz watched her bottom swaying in rhythm with her steps, just as it had swayed earlier to the rhythm of 'Merci Mon Ami.' Like the little fishing boats gently rocking, he thought, and saw her disappear into the wooden barracks that housed the toilets. He went back to the table, sat down and ordered two more mugs of beer.

It was about half an hour before he finally realized that she had left without him. Perhaps she had walked through the garden, screened by the constant bustle of all the customers coming and going; perhaps she had simply slipped out through the rear exit beside the kitchen. At any rate, she was nowhere to be found. He walked up and down the rows of tables several times, asked every single waiter if they had seen her, looked for her indoors in the empty dining areas, and even entered the ladies' toilet, to indignant screeches from its occupants. But the Bohemian girl had gone.

He gulped down the beer, which was warm by now; slurring, he called for the bill and left the beer garden, where the music had started up again a while ago and couples locked in close embrace were swaying in time to 'What Is It Beats So Softly In Your Breast?' Head hanging, hands buried deep in his trouser pockets, he walked through the stream of fairground visitors, which was already considerably thinner than before, and only raised his eyes again when he stood directly underneath the Giant Ferris Wheel. With his few remaining coins he bought a ticket and climbed into the last cabin, the only customer for the last circuit of the evening. As the gondola set off, jerking slightly, and rose slowly up into the air, the light-dappled city unfurled beneath him. The bustling Prater far below. There was St Stephen's Cathedral. The Votive Church over there. In the distance was the Kahlenberg, a dark, hilly outline against the night sky. Franz laid his cheek on a worn wooden window frame and closed his eyes. And when the cabin reached the highest point and the wheel stood still for a moment and Franz felt the gentle rocking beneath his feet and heard the wind whistling outside, he clenched his fist, drew it back, and punched the boards of the cabin so hard that two doves that had settled down hours ago to sleep on the gondola roof flew up in alarm and vanished in the dark expanse of the night.

The next morning, in his little back room, Franz was woken by an unaccustomed racket. Outside, the shop door was wrenched open and slammed shut again several times, bells jangling madly, and there was furious shouting. Franz recognized Otto Trsnyek's angry voice, interrupted by the hoarse bass of the master butcher, Rosshuber, and repeatedly drowned out by the hooting of a small crowd. He climbed out of bed and slipped on his clothes as fast as his pitiable state would allow. His head hurt, and the knuckles of his right hand were painfully swollen. The memory of the previous evening stared back at him from the mirror, pale and hollow of cheek. He spluttered into his wash bucket, gargled with soapy water, dried his face and went outside. A small mob had gathered in front of the tobacconist's, and in the middle Otto Trsnyek and the master butcher were squaring up like a pair of fairground wrestlers.

'Oh, have you come crawling out as well?' the tobacconist yelled at him.

'What's going on?' stammered Franz.

'Open your eyes!' Otto Trsnyek's face was crimson; the veins writhed on his temple like a little pile of bluish worms. Shaking with fury, he pointed one of his crutches at the tobacconist's. The pavement and the shop front were daubed with a reddish-brown liquid. It looked as if someone had splashed it with several buckets of paint or muck. Large, dripping letters on the shop window spelled GET OUT JEWLOVER!, while emblazoned on the wall beside the shop entrance was a round shape, scrawled clumsily and in obvious haste, but clearly recognizable nonetheless as an enormous human posterior with rudimentary features: a so-called 'arse-face'.

Franz stepped over to the window and cautiously touched the J of JEWLOVER with his finger. The graffiti seemed to have been applied with a coarse brush, and had a horrible feel to it — dry and crusted at the edges, still sticky and damp where it was thicker. It also exuded a disgusting smell: rancid, sickly-sweet, but slightly sour as well.

'What is this?' he asked quietly.

'Blood!' yelled Otto Trsnyek. 'Pig's blood! Daubed there by our dear neighbour Rosshuber himself!'

'I'd like to see you prove it,' said the master butcher calmly.

'Besides, that's not sow's blood, it's chicken's. Anyone can see that!'

'Chicken's, then, for all I care!' Otto Trsnyek exploded. 'And who handles these creatures all day long? And who's brainless enough to paint their own self-portrait next to my front door? And who's been wearing the swastika under his lapel for half his life already and can't wait for a chance to turn it outwards?'

'What I wear under my collar is none of your damn business,' said Rosshuber, crossing his massive arms over his chest. 'And the portrait is of the right person!'

'And your hand?' roared Otto Trsnyek.

'What about it?'

'It's still sticky with blood!'

'What else is it going to be sticky with? I'm a butcher, after all!'

Otto Trsnyek gulped. For a moment it looked as if he was going to drop his crutches and fly at the butcher's throat. Suddenly, though, he turned to the circle of people standing around, which had closed in around the commotion and had swelled to quite a sizeable crowd.

'This person!' he began. 'This so-called butcher — whom, incidentally, it would be far more accurate to call a sausage doctorer because he bulks up his sausages by stuffing them with old fat and sawdust — this so-called person and sausage doctorer has blood on his hands. He also has shit for brains and black malice in his heart. And, looking around, he's not alone in that. So far it's only a sow that's had to meet its maker. Or a couple of chickens; whatever. So far it's only a tobacconist's shop that's been defiled. But I'm asking you here, today: what, or who, will be next?'

No one said anything. Some people grinned, some shook their heads, someone left, others joined the crowd and pushed their way through the curious bystanders.

'One man has blood on his hands, and the others stand there and say nothing. That's how it always is!' Otto Trsnyek continued. Rosshuber stood next to him, smiling crookedly. 'That's how it always is, that's how it's always been, and that's how it will always be, because that's probably how it's written somewhere, and that's how it's been instilled into the infinitely stupid human head. But not in mine, ladies and gentlemen! My head still thinks for itself. I won't dance at your party. I don't pin a swastika under my lapel, I don't doctor sausages, I don't sneak about on the pavement in the dark daubing arse-faces on innocent houses, I don't stay silent, and there's no blood on my hands — the only thing you might find there is printer's ink!'

Suddenly all his energy seemed to leave him. His head drooped between his shoulders and he stared down at the pavement. For a few seconds there was silence outside the shop. Only the handles of the crutches could be heard quietly creaking as Otto Trsnyek's fingers clenched around them. At last he gathered himself and, together with a long-drawn-out breath, straightened up again, turned to the butcher and, along with a few flecks of spittle, spat out his concluding words: 'And another thing, Rosshuber. In 1917 I left one of my legs in a mud-filled hole on behalf of our country. This one is all I have. It's old, it's pretty stiff at the hip, and it sometimes feels a wee bit lonely — but it's still enough to give someone a good kick up the arse if necessary!'

With that he left the butcher and all the other people standing and disappeared into his shop with two vigorous swings on his crutches. The door slammed behind him so hard that the windows rattled and the jangling of the bells reached an almost tumultuous crescendo.

In the weeks that followed these events Franz travelled back to the Prater again and again, looking for the girl. He wandered the streets and alleyways for hours, sat in taverns or loitered in front of the swingboats, always in the hope of seeing the face with the straw-blonde hair rise up somewhere in front of him. In vain. Recently it had grown quite uncomfortable, too. Winter had arrived earlier than usual this year: the first snowflakes mingled with the cold drizzle, the rides soon lay under a thick blanket of snow, and one after another had to close down. Only a couple of stalls, the taverns and the pony carousel defied the snow and the cold. Franz stood freezing in front of the little arena and envied the horses, which had now grown woolly winter coats and, untroubled by love and other aberrations, continued to stamp their circles into the cold sand.

At night he often lay awake for hours, thinking about the gap in the Bohemian girl's teeth and tossing and turning with the heat of his own body. If he did eventually find the sleep he longed for, he was immediately beset by turbulent dreams. Pig's blood dripped from the ceiling straight into the round barrel that was his skull; the bed swung higher and higher, out on that sunlight shriek of delight, through an immense black gap, then on, in a little blue wagon, into the eternal darkness of the grotto. His mother appeared and stroked Otto Trsnyek's leg with the back of her hand, which made Sigmund Freud laugh so heartily that his hat flew off his head and he spread his wings and sailed away high above the Votive Church following the setting sun.

If it got too bad, Franz would slip out of the shop through the little door to the back courtyard and walk aimlessly through the streets, until he heard the clip-clopping of the milk carts and the winter dawn was breaking over the frozen roofs. These walks in the silent, nocturnal streets soothed him: he heard the snow crunch beneath his feet and saw his breath drift in front of his face like a delicate little flag. In the early morning twilight, when the lamplighters were climbing their ladders to put out the gas lamps and the first workers were setting off for the early shift with shadowed faces, he found himself in a nebulous limbo between waking and dreaming. And at such times, as he crept back to the tobacconist's, slow and tired, he would see the Bohemian girl on every corner. Bohemian girl under the lantern. Bohemian girl behind the fence. Bohemian girl in the doorway of a house, face illuminated by the glow of a cigarette. Bohemian girl in a shop window, stretching out her arms to him and laughing.

Postcard of Schönbrunn Palace gardens, lamplit and sugar-frosted with snow.

> *Dear Mother,*
> *I've been here in the city for quite a while now, yet to be honest it seems to me that everything just gets stranger. But maybe it's like that all through life — from the moment you're born, with every single day, you grow a little bit further away from yourself until one day you don't know where you are any more. Can that really be the way it is?*
> *With best wishes,*
> *Your Franz*

Postcard of the Attersee, green and shimmering like a jewel, clearly taken from an aeroplane or Zeppelin.

> *Dear Franzl,*
> *Have you fallen in love, I wonder? Because that would be one explanation for the way you're feeling. It's well known that falling in love means you don't know where you are any more. As far as your question is concerned, I can tell you that all of life is perpetual*

parting. A mother knows that only too well. But that's just the way it is, and you get used to it. I hope you are well otherwise and that you're not discrediting Otto Trsnyek. Here at the lake there's no news for the time being, and that's actually quite nice.
Sending you a big hug,
Your Mama

'You look terrible,' said Otto Trsnyek, without looking up from his bookkeeping.

'What?' asked Franz, confused. He lifted his head, which had sunk onto his chest again. Two months had passed since he had found happiness in the Prater and promptly lost it again. Two months of gloomy days and sleepless nights.

'I said you look terrible!' repeated Otto Trsnyek. 'Godawful, to be precise. Like Death's own grandfather. White as a sheet, thin as a rake, dog-tired, and a good ten years older than your age. If you carry on like this you can start drawing your pension next year.'

'No, no, I'm fine,' said Franz quickly, bending to pick up the paper that had slipped from his listless hands. 'I'm finding the weather a bit difficult, I suppose, but everything's all right apart from that.'

'What's wrong with the weather?'

'It's . . . a bit cold.'

'It's winter.'

'Yes,' sighed Franz quietly. 'Winter.'

The tobacconist peered over the rim of his glasses at his apprentice, who was now trying to bury his head in the Business section.

'And apart from the extremely unusual fact that winter is already upon us in December this year, what else is troubling you?'

It took a few seconds for Franz to abandon his resistance, but then he finally allowed the newspaper to slide to the floor, leaped up from the stool and shouted at the dusty ceiling in despair: 'I've fallen in love!'

In the briefest of moments, about half as long as it takes to skim a headline, Otto Trsnyek grasped the seriousness of the situation. 'Jesus, Mary and Joseph,' he exclaimed, 'that's bad!'

'Worse than bad!' cried Franz. 'It's a disaster! What on earth do I do now?'

Otto Trsnyek considered. Eventually he shrugged. 'I have no idea. Go to the swimming pool and swim a few lengths. That's good for the bones and clears the head!'

Franz lowered his hands and looked at him. For the first time he noticed how small the tobacconist was. It was as if he had shrunk in recent weeks. Soon he would have dissolved entirely in the dusty shadow of his stack of newspapers.

'The swimming pool?'

Otto Trsnyek scratched himself behind the right ear. His gaze travelled slowly across the sales counter, slid over the edge, down to the ground, and crept across the floorboards in little arcs before finally getting stuck somewhere just in front of Franz's toecaps.

'Listen, I don't understand these things any more. Maybe I used to, when I still had something going for me in that regard. Ask your mother, she'll probably remember. But that's a long time ago. Half a lifetime. The truth is, I left my youth behind in the trenches along with my leg. That's the way it is. Sometimes it's painful, but to be honest it has its upsides, too. Love can't do anything to me any more. I've got my peace and quiet as far as that's concerned, and if I want to get het up I read the newspaper. There's enough senselessness in the world, I don't need that kind of thing in my shop as well. So if I might give you a modest piece of advice, my awkward young apprentice: in delicate matters such as these, look for another confidant, and don't bring your problems to me.'

He gave a slightly embarrassed smile, then blew carefully on the nib of his fountain pen to dry it and bent low over his books. After a while Franz sat down again, and neither of them said anything else for the rest of the day.

At Berggasse 19 the most wonderful aromas lingered in the air. It smelled of savoury pancake soup, roast beef and onions in gravy with parsley potatoes, and vanilla pudding in a hot dark chocolate sauce, sprinkled with freshly roasted flaked almonds. Professor Sigmund Freud removed his napkin, surreptitiously undid the top button of his trousers and folded his hands on his stomach with a contented groan. Just this once — and only because Martha, the professor's wife, was in bed two rooms away with a slight temperature and a nasty dry cough — his daughter Anna had done the cooking this Sunday. Over the years Anna had become not only an immensely productive and empathetic psychoanalyst (and more: her father's only legitimate successor and a loyal champion of his work), but also — a fact of which Freud was secretly almost more appreciative — a proficient and talented cook. In particular, roast beef and onions was a dish she prepared better than almost anyone in Vienna: the meat was succulent and cooked to a turn, the onions sautéed golden yellow in flour and butter, and the potatoes sprinkled with tiny snippets of freshly chopped parsley. Freud looked at his daughter out of the corner of his eye. She was still prodding at her pudding with her little silver spoon while leafing through one of Arthur Schopenhauer's thickest tomes. She had rolled her hair up into two snail-like coils at the back of her head, and these were illuminated by a couple of rays of the winter sun that, for a few midday minutes, had strayed down the urban canyon of Berggasse all the way into the Freud family dining room. It had always been a mystery to him where women found the dexterity and patience to construct such edifices upon their heads. From the bedroom came the sound of someone quietly clearing their throat, followed by a comfortable groan and a few indefinable noises from the bed. Ah, Woman, thought Freud, in silent wonder. What does she want, and what's it all about?

At that moment he sensed Anna looking at him, a look he loved more than anything else in the world. 'I'd better take another peek,' she said. She set spoon and Schopenhauer aside, went to the window and glanced down into the street.

'He's still there!'

Freud gave a little cough. 'How long has he been sitting down there now?'

'About three hours.'

'In this cold?'

'He's got a scarf.'

Freud gingerly explored his prosthetic jaw with the tip of his tongue. That sharp edge at the back needed a bit of smoothing, and the side corner would have to be polished slightly. While he was eating the pain in his mouth had been bearable, but it was slowly worsening again. The truth was that none of the eminent doctors were any good. Maybe he should see a carpenter next time. Or go straight to a tombstone carver. He stared for a while into the middle distance, expressionless. A solitary sliver of almond lay on the tablecloth beside the breadbasket. He tapped it with his fingertip and popped it in his mouth. Then, with a sigh that seemed to encompass the pain of all mankind, he rose and said, 'I will smoke outside today!'

Franz leaped to his feet the instant the heavy door swung open and the professor stepped outside. The momentum of his fervour almost knocked him down again: his legs were as stiff as boards, and his bottom ached from the hours of sitting on the cold wooden bench. Now, though, he stood and watched as the professor, slightly bent over as usual, crossed the street on rather unsteady legs and walked straight over to him.

'May I sit down?' asked Freud, sinking onto the bench without waiting for an answer. With his fingertips he fished a little matte silver box from his coat pocket and took out a Virginia. But before he could stick the cheroot between his lips Franz was already sitting beside him, holding a long, slim cigar under his nose. The professor swallowed. 'A Hoyo de Monterrey,' he said, huskily.

Franz nodded. 'Harvested by brave men on the sunny, fertile banks of the San Juan y Martínez River and tenderly hand-rolled by their beautiful women.'

Freud gently palpated the cigar along its entire length and squeezed it lightly between thumb and forefinger.

'An aromatic *habano* that is light in taste, yet persuades through great elegance and complexity,' said Franz, with a naturalness that gave no hint of the many painstaking hours it had cost him to learn the descriptions on the cigar box by heart. He took a silver-plated cigar cutter from the pocket of his trousers and handed it to the professor. 'A *habano* should be cut precisely on the line — here, where cap and wrapper join.'

Freud cut off the end and lit the Hoyo with a match as long as his finger. In doing so he held the flame about a centimetre away from the tip and drew on the cigar until the flame reached it. Then he turned it slowly between his fingers and blew softly on the embers. He leaned back with a faint smile and gazed at the bluish smoke curling up and away in the clear winter air.

'Now then. Out with it. What do you want?'

Franz cleared his throat awkwardly, shifted about on the bench, cleared his throat again, and finally turned to the man sitting beside him with the despairing face of a drowning man.

'I'm in love, Herr Professor!'

Freud held his cigar up to the light and contemplated it thoughtfully.

'Congratulations!' he said. 'You don't lose any time, do you?'

'No, Herr Professor, but I've lost *her*!'

'Who?'

'The girl!'

'I thought you were in love?'

'Yes, but unhappily!' The words burst out of Franz like a cork from a shaken champagne bottle.

Freud, whose prosthetic jaw was starting to torment him again, put his head to one side and stared for a while into the empty space between the bench and the front door of his house. '*Ut desint vires, tamen est laudanda voluntas,*' he said at last, and it sounded as if he was trying to grind each word individually between his teeth.

'Excuse me, Herr Professor?'

'It means something along the lines of "Chin up!"'

'How can such a long sentence have such a short meaning?'

'That's often the way with sentences. People who talk a lot usually don't have much to say,' Freud answered, rather morosely. 'Besides, what exactly have I got to do with all this?'

'It's your fault!' cried Franz. 'You told me to enjoy myself and find myself a girl!'

'So now the doctor is the pathogen from which the disease arises?'

'Oh, really!' Franz leaped to his feet and began to stride up and down in front of the bench. 'I don't understand anything about doctors or pathogens. All I know is that I'm aroused! Permanently and all the time. I can hardly work. I can hardly sleep. I dream stupid things. I run around town until the sun comes up. I'm hot. I'm cold. I'm sick. I've got a stomach ache, headache, heartache. All at once. Not long ago I was still sitting on the shore of the lake watching the ducks. Then I arrive in town and immediately everything goes haywire. And it's not just in me: it's everywhere else as well. You can read about it in the papers. One day everyone's shouting for this Schuschnigg, the next day everyone's shouting for this Hitler. And I'm sitting in the tobacconist's asking myself: who are these two, anyway? I clean pig's blood off the shop window and sit bawling in the grotto train. I dance with the most beautiful girl in the world, and the next minute she's gone. Vanished. Was never there. So I'm asking you: have I gone mad? Or has the whole world gone mad?'

Professor Freud flicked the ash off his Hoyo with his fore-finger and blew delicately on the embers. 'First of all, sit back down,' he said calmly. 'Secondly, yes, the world has gone mad. And thirdly, have no illusions, it's going to get a lot madder than this.'

Franz dropped back onto the bench and stared ominously into space. 'Basically, I don't care whether or not the world tears itself off its hinges. The only thing that interests me is this girl.'

'What's her name, anyway?'

'Don't know.'

'You don't even know her name?'

'I don't really know anything about her at all. Except that she's Bohemian. And her teeth have the most beautiful gap in the world.'

'The most beautiful gap? It sounds as if you've really got it bad.'

'Told you.'

'So what do you expect from me?'

'You're a doctor! And a professor, too.'

'Yes, and?'

'You've written books. Lots of books! Isn't there anything at all in there that can help me?'

'To be honest, I don't think there is.'

'What's the point of all the books, then?'

'I sometimes ask myself the same question.' Freud drew in his feet, pushed his hat a little lower on his forehead and turned up his collar with one hand. They sat beside each other without speaking as he took a few more puffs on the cigar. The sun had disappeared behind the roofs and it had got colder on the bench. Franz saw that the professor's hand trembled slightly when he raised the cigar to his lips. His skin was mottled and stretched as thin as tissue paper over the sinews. Only now did it occur to Franz how old and frail Freud was. He unwound his scarf from his neck and handed it to the professor.

'What am I supposed to do with it?' the old man growled.

'It's winter — you mustn't play with your health!'

'Ha!' barked Freud, his voice tinged with bitter merriment. 'I'm too old to stop playing!'

'No one is too old for my mother's hand-knitted woollen scarf,' Franz countered sternly, and with an elegant movement he wrapped it round the Professor's skinny neck. After a moment of frozen incredulity, Freud stretched his chin up out of the thick wool and busied himself again with the cigar, which had shrunk to almost half its length.

'So this young lady stood you up,' he murmured to himself. 'That's the fact of the matter. In my view you now have precisely two options. Option number one: go and get her back! Option number two: forget her!'

'That's it?'

'That's it.'

'Please excuse me, Herr Professor, but if all your advice is like this, I don't understand why people pay so much money to be allowed to lie on your couch.'

Freud sighed. For a fraction of a second he considered yielding to the sense of anger that was welling up deep inside, and stubbing out his Hoyo on the brow of this impertinent country lad. He decided against it, and puffed smoke rings into the air instead.

'People pay so much money precisely because they *don't* get to hear any advice from me. And perhaps I should remind you that *you* are the one who's been loitering outside my front door for three hours on the Lord's day to seek my advice and bribe me with an admittedly excellent cigar.'

'Because I'm desperate!'

'Yes, yes,' sighed Freud, 'even the best of us are dashed to pieces on the rocks of the Feminine.'

'And I'm certainly not one of the best.'

'That remains to be seen,' said the professor, looking up at the dining room window, where Anna had appeared with raised and threatening forefinger, an unmistakable indication that he should come back inside now, at once, immediately, into the warm.

'Is that your daughter?'

The professor nodded. Franz looked up at Anna and greeted her with the widest smile of which his frozen cheeks were capable. She raised her hand immediately in a little wave, then quickly tweaked the curtains straight and disappeared behind them.

'She looks a bit like my mother. From a distance, I mean.'

'Do you really have to remind me that I'm as old as Methuselah?' grumbled Freud. He closed his eyes and took a last, concentrated puff on his Hoyo; but it was over. The taste of the cigar scarcely compensated any more for the pain in his mouth. Carefully he set the burning stump down on the arm-rest and watched as the embers slowly faded.

'Thus it departs in peace,' he murmured as it went out, and Franz nodded. They looked at each other.

'Now what?' asked Franz.

'Now I'm going to write you a prescription,' Freud replied, 'or rather, three prescriptions. And although it might sound a bit paradoxical, I'm going to write these prescriptions ver-bally. So listen carefully, and make sure you remember them! First prescription (for your headache): stop thinking about love. Second prescription (for your stomach ache and confus-ing dreams): put paper and pen by your bed and write down all your dreams as soon as you wake up. Third prescription (for your heartache): get the girl back — or forget her!'

The sun had long since vanished. The cold wind blew a few scraps of newspaper down Berggasse. Someone opened a window; music escaped for a moment, a marching band of some sort, then all was quiet again. The Professor gathered himself, with an effort, and they both stood up.

'I wish you luck, Franz!' he said, and held out his hand. Franz felt the old man's fingers in his, as thin and light as brushwood.

'I'll need it.'

Freud had already crossed the street and was in the process of taking the house keys out of his coat pocket when Franz's voice, by now trembling with cold, reached him again. 'May I lie on your couch as well sometime, Herr Professor?'

Freud turned around.

'What do you want to lie on the couch for?'

'Don't know. I'll find out when I get to lie on it.'

Freud stared at the boy in disbelief. He pushed his hat back off his forehead and twisted his beard between two fingers.

'First the prescriptions — and then we'll see. All right?'

'All right.'

For a few seconds they were silent. Eventually Freud twisted his mouth into a crooked smile and put the key in the lock.

'Merry Christmas, Franz!'

'Merry Christmas, Herr Professor!'

The tobacconist's was closed over the Christmas period. Otto Trsnyek had entrusted both the keys and the responsibility for its silent rooms to Franz, and had gone to visit a second cousin in Potzneusiedl to 'treat my soul and my leg to a little peace and quiet in Burgenlandish ennui'. Franz spent most of the time in his little room, mustering his strength for the forth-coming re-conquest, on the one hand; on the other, because ever since that Sunday afternoon on the wooden bench he had been plagued by a vicious cold. Outside, it had been snowing non-stop for days. The municipal clearance teams, consisting of the emaciated unemployed and Austrian Army soldiers with the baby faces of country boys, had piled the snow halfway up the shop window. Inside the tobacconist's it was dim and silent, and Franz had plenty of peace and quiet. Mostly he lay in bed and passed the time listening to the soft explosions of the coal stove and thinking about the gap in those Bohemian teeth. On Christmas Eve he lit a candle and polished off the entire contents of a parcel his mother had sent him, filled to the brim with vanilla crescent biscuits, deep-fried doughnuts, jam pastries and other floury delights that smelled of home and childhood. At the bottom of the box Franz found a little photograph. It showed his mother standing on the icy surface of the snow-covered Attersee. She was wearing one of her hand-knitted bobble hats, a woollen jacket, a winter skirt and her old traditional shoes, thickly lined with rabbit fur. She was looking straight at the camera and laughing. One arm was stretched out in front of her; it seemed to be pointing somewhere, perhaps towards the cottage, or perhaps beyond, to the fog-shrouded peak of the Schafberg. The photo had almost certainly been taken by Sieglmeier, the parish priest. The priest was one of the few people in Nussdorf in possession of a camera, and Franz's mother had probably bribed him with a spicy fish soup, fresh strudels, or a promise to attend church regularly. Now a solitary tear fell onto the photograph, leaving a damp, round mark precisely where his mother's arm projected into the sky. Franz quickly wiped his thumb across it and turned the picture over. Written on the back, in pale blue crayon, was the message:

My dear Franzl,
I wish you with all my heart a happy Christmas and blessed New
Year.
Your Mama
PS: Are you still in love?
PPS: If your trousers are dirty, you can send them to me.
PPPS: Stop calling me 'Mother', I'm your Mama and that's that.

Franz selected a particularly impressive card from the stand (a statue of Johann Strauss with a crown of snow on his head, surrounded by the Vienna Boys' Choir) and wrote in his best fountain-pen script:

Dear Mama,
Christmas is almost over again, and I've eaten every single thing
in your parcel. The last few weeks have been a bit of a strain, but
I'm sure everything will sort itself out again in the New Year.
Your Franzl
PS: I'm still in love.
PPS: My trousers aren't dirty.
PPPS: All right then.

Franz finally recovered from his cold and fever in time for New Year's Eve. He headed for Annagasse in the centre of town where, amid hundreds of Viennese in a 'world-famous and highly regarded dance establishment' (as promised in the advertisements cleverly placed in a number of newspapers), he welcomed in the new year by downing a two-litre bottle of vinegary white burgundy that he'd smuggled in under his shirt, and waltzing with a fat woman. Early the next day, the first of the hopeful new year 1938, he boarded the tram and trundled through the blizzard towards the Prater. The Giant Ferris Wheel loomed up in the sky, dark and still, and the rides lay as if dead and buried beneath a thick blanket of snow. The alleyways were almost deserted, with just the occasional disorientated pedestrian trudging around between the stalls. Glittering icicles hung on the great swingboat, and a crow squatted on the topmost cabin, hacking at the snow with its beak. Franz went over to the Schweizerhaus, where the lights were already burning and the snow had been shovelled away from the entrance in preparation for the first lunchtime of the year. He entered the bar room and went straight up to the moustachioed waiter, who was standing, heavy-lidded, behind the counter, examining a freshly-polished glass in the dim light of the ceiling lamps.

Could he be of any assistance to the young gentleman, the waiter asked, without looking at him. Maintaining a bored expression, Franz looked around the room while casually pushing a banknote across the counter. He had a question, he said, a small thing really, quickly asked and even more quickly answered.

It must be a really tiny little thing, said the waiter, if the value on this scrap of paper was anything to go by. Silently, Franz took another note from his jacket pocket and placed it beside the first. The waiter put the glass back on the shelf and slipped the money into his apron.

Come on, he said.

Outside it was snowing even harder now. Thick white flakes sank noiselessly from the sky, settling in their hair and catching on their eyelashes. Franz and the waiter sought shelter under a big chestnut tree.

What exactly was this small thing, the waiter wanted to know.

It was about one of his compatriots, said Franz. A Bohemian girl.

Just because he spoke Czech, the waiter said, that didn't make him a Bohemian, to make that quite clear. There was a soft rustling in the treetop overhead; a handful of snow fell gently to the ground.

At any rate, said Franz, he was sure the gentleman remembered that, not all that long ago, he and this Bohemian girl had had a couple of beers and danced right underneath this chestnut tree. She was very beautiful. Quite plump, with hair as blonde as the sun, a delicately puckered upper lip, and a gap in her teeth that could have been sculpted by the hand of God.

The waiter shrugged. A tricky business, memory, he said, staring sadly at the little mound of snow on his toecaps. Franz sighed and drew another banknote from his coat pocket.

Oh yes, said the waiter; funny, but he did remember now, there was this fat Bohemian girl.

Plump, said Franz. Plump, not fat.

If you say so, said the waiter. What about her?

Her address, answered Franz. Did the gentleman have an address for her? Or her name. Or anything. He certainly knew her, anyway; that much had been obvious.

As a Prater waiter one knew a lot of people, the waiter replied. It was hard to say.

Franz stuck his last banknote in the waiter's apron. Perhaps that made it a little easier?

The waiter smiled. Why did it have to be such a porky little peasant, he wanted to know. After all, there were other, quite different opportunities to be had in the Prater; he was sure something could be arranged.

Plump, said Franz, staring fixedly at him. Plump, not porky.

Plump, porky, it was just a question of definition, said the waiter. But either way, cheap was cheap.

At that, something snapped in Franz. With a stifled cry he hurled himself at the waiter and started to punch him. The moustache ducked away, bobbed two steps to the side, one back, one forward again, and threw a straight jab, quick as a flash. The blow caught Franz high on the bridge of his nose; there was a hollow sound and a shadow descended on him, cloaking everything in darkness and silence.

Seconds later, Franz regained consciousness. He was lying on his back looking straight into the waiter's moustachioed face looming over him.

He was a bit out of practice, the waiter told him good-naturedly, but it would just about do for any country bumpkins who happened to come along. Should he help him up?

No thank you, answered Franz, and stayed where he was.

The waiter said that where women were concerned there was no need to resort to violence straight away.

No, there probably wasn't, said Franz.

The waiter gave him stern, paternal look. Really — how stupid of him!

Franz nodded. Could he perhaps get her address or name now, after all?

Stubborn as a Styrian ox, said the waiter, shaking his head.

An Upper Austrian one, said Franz, as the sweet taste of blood began to fill his mouth.

If you say so, said the waiter. A light dusting of snow had begun to settle on his thick hair, giving him a grandfatherly look. The babble of his colleagues' voices issued from the bar. Laughter. Someone broke into song. Then all was quiet again. The waiter sighed.

Not far from here, in the second district, he said. The yellow house on Rotensterngasse. Just follow the rats: rubbish

heap to the left, rubbish heap to the right. The young gentleman could try looking there, if he absolutely must.

Thank you, said Franz.

You're welcome, said the waiter. He jumped up and down
a few times, smacked the snow from his shoulders and ran his
fingers through his moustache. Hopefully there'd be an end to
this shitty weather soon; it couldn't carry on like this.

Franz nodded.

Now he really did have to go back in, said the waiter; there
couldn't be much point in standing around under a chestnut
tree in the snow all day.

Right, said Franz, goodbye.

Goodbye.

After the waiter had disappeared into the bar, Franz lay there
a while longer, gazing up into the whirling snow. It soon seemed
to him that it wasn't the snowflakes that were flying towards him,
but he who was rising up from the ground and hurtling away
ever faster, higher and higher, up into the wide and silent sky.

The yellow house on Rotensterngasse was a ruin, ripe for dem-
olition. As the waiter had said, to the left and right of the
entrance were rubbish heaps several metres high. The plaster
was falling off the façade; the windows were either grey with
dust or had boards nailed across them. Brownish icicles hung
from the gutter, and the words SCHUSCHNIGG YOU JEWISH DOG!
were scrawled across one of the cellar windows in green paint.

The front door stood wide open, but in spite of this it was dark in the hallway and stank of damp walls and urine. There was something else in the air, too: a sharp, sweetish smell that wafted towards Franz like a distant memory of home. It smelled of pigsty. Franz couldn't help smiling to himself. Cautiously he ascended the staircase; little lumps of mortar crunched beneath his feet, and with every stair the stench grew more pungent. At home it wouldn't have bothered anyone, he thought, certainly not him. Generally speaking, the pigs stank less than forestry workers after their shift, for example, or schoolchildren after a sports lesson. He himself had even crawled into the neighbouring farmers' pigsties from time to time, had cuddled the piglets like little pink brothers and snuggled up beside them in the straw. Here, though, inside these grey city walls, the smell was unseemly and disgusting. On the mezzanine floor one of the doors had come off its hinges, and in the room beyond he spotted the pig. It was a massive animal; heavy and motionless it lay on the straw-strewn tiled floor, snuffling quietly. Beside it, on a fruit crate, sat an old woman. She had a saucepan in her lap in which she was slowly and steadily mixing dough.

'Excuse me, does a young woman live here, by any chance, from Bohemia?' asked Franz.

The old woman stared at him for a moment, then pointed silently at the ceiling with her spoon. A rubbery lump of dough peeled off and plopped into her lap. The sow heaved itself over onto its other side, raised its head and gazed dully at the wall.

On the second floor most of the apartments seemed to be empty: almost all the doors stood open or were missing altogether. Only the door of the last apartment, right at the end of the corridor, was intact. An indistinct babble could be heard behind it. Franz knocked twice and it immediately fell silent. He heard brief whispers, then a high voice said, 'Come in!' Franz wiped the remnants of snow from his collar, took a deep breath and opened the door.

As far as he could tell at first glance, there were about thirty women in the room. They sat at little tables, on chairs, crates, buckets. Three were perched next to one another on the window ledge like birds on a bough. Some were bedded down on old mattresses ranged along the walls. Two young girls sat cross-legged in front of a low charcoal stove, playing cards; a woman stood before a shard of mirror on the wall, making up her eyes with a stick of charcoal; another sat on an upturned laundry basket, clasping a tiny child to her breast.

'Excuse me,' said Franz timidly, 'does a young woman live here, by any chance, from Bohemia?' One of the girls giggled; another, with blue eyes like water, put her hand over her mouth and stifled a laugh. The others just sat and stared at him.

'Ah, is sonny boy with nice ass!'

He recognised her voice immediately. She was sitting on a mattress, her knees drawn up, wrapped in a thin woollen blanket. Her hair had disappeared beneath a kerchief and her face was almost entirely shadowed by the blanket. But even so,

Franz knew that she was smiling. And now he was smiling, too. And if the Bohemian girl in her woollen blanket hadn't released him from his happy stupor with the words, 'You can pay me meal and glass of wine, sonny boy!' he would probably have gone on standing in the doorway for the rest of the afternoon, or beyond, smiling a smile that looked as if it could embrace the whole world, or at the very least these thirty women in their damp hovel.

She was called Anezka, and she was three years older than him. She came from a 'very beautiful willage' called Dobrovice ('curled up to hill Viničný like to dark lover') in the district of Mladá Boleslav, and worked variously as a nursemaid, cook or domestic help — without an official permit, like all the other women in the yellow house. 'All Bohemian. Lovely, good woman, every one!'

They crunched along side by side through the snow-covered streets, and Franz told her about home, where the lake changed colour with the seasons: in spring it was dark green, in summer silver, in autumn dark blue, and in winter black as the devil's heart. And he told her about the cows whose cowpats were so big a child could sink into them up to its knees, and about the fish he had pulled from the water as a little boy that were so fat a single one was enough to satisfy an entire brigade of woodcutters. He described the pleasure steamers that thumped across the water every day in summer with their colourful, chaotic crowds of tourists on deck and children swimming after them as they cast off, trying to race them. And he described for her his mother's potato strudel, famous throughout the whole of the Salzkammergut: how in the winter months she would knead the dough on the table before frying it in goose fat in the big iron pan and piling it up in a golden-yellow, steaming, fragrant mountain. Franz told her about these and about other, quite different things. The words poured out of him, unfurling before them in such a wonderful panorama that they went on walking through the almost deserted streets until night fell and the gas workers climbed their ladders, brushed the snow caps from the lanterns, and lights began to shimmer all around them through the blizzard.

Anezka stopped at a little tavern. 'We eat now!' she said, and went in. Franz ordered two portions of goulash and a bottle of foreign wine that was so good even the waiter couldn't pronounce its name. The goulash was hot and spicy, the gherkins snapped, and the bread rolls crackled. Franz had never seen someone eat with such abandon. And he had never been so happy to watch someone eat. He ordered a second helping, then a third. Afterwards there were pancakes with chocolate sauce and a thick layer of icing sugar, and a second bottle of wine. When the last specks of pancake had finally been washed down with the last mouthful of wine, Anezka leaned back with a long-drawn-out sigh, crossed her hands over her belly and gazed languidly at Franz.

'And now I want you, sonny boy!' she said.

The shop floor was silent, bathed in the blue, snowy light that fell through the few gaps on the poster-covered windows. When Franz had closed the front door behind them, Anezka raised her nose, sniffing, deeply inhaling the smell of tobacco and paper. Franz was planning to indicate the way to his little room with a gesture both polite and, at the same time, nonchalant and urbane when he felt her hand on his behind, on the exact same spot where it had lain once before, so very long ago, when they danced in the Schweizerhaus. His heart immediately started hammering like mad, and a fiery heat welled up inside him. He wanted to ask something, something tremendously urgent, something incredibly important, something that was tingling on the tip of his tongue, but already her other hand was on his other buttock and her hip was pushing against his, and the words evaporated in his head like drops on a hot stove. She looked him in the eyes and, very slowly, brought her face up close to his, and when he felt her breath on his mouth and saw the delicate trembling of her puckered top lip, a shudder of joy passed through him with such force that he would almost certainly have fallen backwards into the cigar rack if Anezka hadn't caught him at the last moment and pressed him firmly against her body. He closed his eyes and heard himself make a gurgling sound. And as his trousers slipped down his legs all the burdens of his life to date seemed to fall away from him; he tipped back his head and gazed up into the darkness beneath the ceiling, and for one blessed moment he felt as if

he could understand the things of this world in all their immea-
surable beauty. How strange they are, he thought, life and all
of these things. Then he felt Anezka slide down before him to
the floor, felt her hands grab his naked buttocks and draw him
to her. 'Come, sonny boy!' he heard her whisper, and with a
smile he let go.

And if anybody had, for any reason, been loitering outside
a couple of hours later on that icy night, perhaps they would
have seen the door of the old Trsnyek's tobacconist's fly open
and two naked figures, a thin young man and a plump young
woman, tumble out into the open air, pelt each other, squealing,
with snow for a while, dash a little way down Währingerstrasse
and finally, arms and legs outstretched, fall backwards into a
great heap of snow at about the level of old Frau Sternitzka's
furrier's shop. But of course at that time of night and in that
filthy weather nobody was out on the street. Nobody was there
to see Franz and Anezka lie beside each other, panting, looking
up at the sky. And no one was there to hear the brief conver-
sation Franz initiated with a question that had been buzzing
around his slowly cooling head for some minutes.

'Why did you run away back then, in the Schweizerhaus?'

Anezka stretched her arm up in the air and traced the contours of the surrounding roofs with her finger. It had almost
completely stopped snowing; dark scraps of cloud were scud-
ding across the sky, and the moon shimmered weakly from
behind a chimney.

'Sometimes must run away, sometimes must stay,' she said. 'So is life.'

'Well, maybe . . .' Franz began, in feeble protest, but even as he did so her hand made an elegant turn in mid-air, then swooped down abruptly and with devastating accuracy to seize his cock. 'Not talk so much,' she said, 'better to screw again.' Of course, she didn't say 'screw' but 'scrrrrrrew', with rolling, Bohemian *r*'s. Franz understood her perfectly all the same.

Franz's sexual deliverance did not signify an improvement in his general state of being. A fire had been ignited between his thighs; it burned fiercely and would be impossible to extinguish again, that much was clear to him. At the same time — of this too he had been made painfully aware — there was still so much to learn. The night had been too short; even a whole lifetime seemed insufficient to comprehend the mystery of Woman in all her terrible beauty. 'Even the best among us are dashed to pieces on the rocks of the Feminine', the professor had said. That may be, thought Franz, but if so, then that was just how it was. Let him be dashed to pieces — as long as it was on Anezka's splendid coast. There was no going back now. He wanted to keep going, keep practising, keep learning. He wanted to lie beside her again come what may, with her wonderful scent in his nostrils and her hands on that eager student, his behind.

To that end he set off the very next evening to the yellow house on Rotensterngasse, walked through the stinking hall, up the crumbling staircase, past the old woman with the quietly snuffling pig and up into the apartment, which once again was crammed with Bohemian women. But Anezka wasn't there. Nor the next day, either. Nor the following weekend. Or the one after that. Anezka not here, Anezka out, Anezka gone, Anezka somewhere, Anezka working, said the women who happened to be in the apartment at the time; they never, incidentally, seemed to be the same ones. Where or for whom she worked they couldn't say, didn't know, didn't want to know, and Franz retreated again, with his shining, greasy carefully parted hair and the box of expensive chocolates he had purchased at a specialist confectioner's in town under his arm. During the day he sat on his stool, white as a sheet, and pretended to read the paper. At night he tossed and turned in bed and buried his face in the pillow where, but a short while ago, her hair had fanned out like rays of sunshine. Periods of sleep were short and shot through with confusing dreams. Sometimes he followed the professor's advice and tried to tame this frenzied inner life by writing down his dreams as soon as he awoke. It was no good. It was no help. Nothing helped or were any good. It was as if Anezka had ripped his heart out of his chest and was now carrying it around with her. The thing still beating in his chest was just the memory of what was already in her possession: in her open hand, the pocket of her apron, squashed between the slats of her bed frame, hot and pulsating before her on the kitchen table.

And then it happened after all. A couple of agonizing weeks after the earth first moved at the tobacconist's, Franz was roused from half-sleep in the middle of the night by a quiet knock. Outside stood Anezka in a short coat, freezing. She said nothing. Without a word she walked past him and got into bed. She left it to him to undress her. His hands were shaking so hard it took him forever. Slowly, bit by bit, her body revealed itself until at last she lay before him, naked and soft and plump in the milky radiance of the moonlight. Afterwards, as he lay on his back beside her, a little heap of happiness, he imagined how the following morning, as soon as they got up, he would ask her for her hand. But when he awoke, she was gone.

Franz decided to implement the professor's second proposed solution to the problem and forget Anezka. He tried very hard, but when, after more than three weeks, the prints of her small hands still burned his buttocks, and her name kept flashing up in ghostly fashion between every second line of the newspaper, and when finally the contours of first her puckered top lip, then her face, and lastly her body materialized in the grain of the floorboards as he was wiping up the drips left by Kommerzialrat Ruskovetz's dachshund, he abandoned the forgetting idea. Instead, he tossed the rag into a corner and planted himself in front of Otto Trsnyek, feet apart and hands determinedly on his hips. He was sorry, he said in a very loud voice, but he simply couldn't stand it any more. He had to go to a doctor right now, immediately, this instant, about his spine, which had started to collapse and was all in all quite painfully crooked from all the hours of sitting on the stool. The tobacconist screwed the top on his fountain pen, placed it carefully in its leather case, which had got a little greasy over the years, bent over the piece of paper he had just filled with a list of things that urgently needed ordering, gently blew the ink dry, looked over the top of his glasses at his apprentice, still standing in front of him in the same position, feet apart, and, sighing heavily, dismissed him for the rest of the day with the words: 'Well, clear off, then, if that's what you want!'

Franz, of course, went not to the doctor but straight to the yellow house in the Rotensterngasse, where he sat on a low pile of crumbling bricks behind one of the two rubbish heaps and waited. Nothing happened all afternoon. Women were constantly going in and out, but Anezka wasn't among them. The hours passed: a few rays of sun wandered briefly across the rubbish, it rained a little, after which it grew cold, evening came and darkness fell. Franz felt the dampness of the bricks slowly seeping up through his trousers, and railed silently at himself. What had possessed him to come up with the harebrained idea of listening to some ancient, practically weightless professor — who smelled of sawdust, to boot — and getting caught up in something as idiotic as love? A little later, when the gas man came and lit the street's three functioning lanterns, he finally gave up. There was a smacking sound as he raised his damp behind off the pile of bricks, about to beat a retreat to the tobacconist's. Precisely at that moment, she came out of the house. Her head was slightly bowed; she had turned up the collar of her coat, and she walked down the street with small, quick steps, in the other direction. Franz emerged from behind the rubbish heap and followed her at a safe distance. Just like in the American detective movie he'd seen years ago with his mother at a well-attended screening in St. Georgen, with all those mercilessly grim or dreamily wistful men, he tried to use the intricacies of the urban environment as cover: he ducked into the entrances of buildings, jumped behind an advertising column, crossed the road, ran a little way alongside a diesel truck loaded with steaming tar, and hid behind the broad back of a tired sewer worker trudging home in his heavy thigh boots. Anezka crossed Weintraubengasse, reached Praterstrasse, and moved swiftly and surely through the thick traffic towards the Giant Ferris Wheel. Behind the Grand Autodrome she suddenly turned right and disappeared down a small, dark side street. Franz waited a few seconds, and then he too turned into the alley. The street was narrow and bordered on both sides by an unusually high fence: the planks loomed up, leaving only a strip of the starless night sky at the top. After about twenty paces the passageway opened out onto a rear courtyard enclosed by dirty walls. A couple of dustbins stood in one corner, huddled together like sleeping cows. A light bulb dangled from a naked wire, dispensing its

dirty yellow light. Out of the corner of his eye Franz caught a
movement in the semi-darkness of an alcove, soft and silent,
like a languid wave. It was the fold of a curtain moving in
a draught. Above it, a poster stuck on the wall read TO THE
GROTTO in dull gold letters. Underneath, barely legible: COME
CLOSER! COME INSIDE! SECRET PLEASURE, ALONE OR TOGETHER,
COME SAMPLE OUR DELIGHTS! (ENTRY ONE SCHILLING)

Franz pushed aside the curtain and went in. The room
was tiny and completely immersed in dark green light. He
was reminded of the lake, of dives he had made so often as a
boy: the countless hot summer days when he had lain naked
on one of the fishing jetties that smelled of wood and sunshine, listening to the rustling of the reeds and the friendly
lapping of the water beneath him, until it became irresistible
and he had to hurl himself in, headfirst or clutching his knees.
Slowly he would let himself sink amid the swirling of his own
air bubbles, and around him it would grow ever quieter and
darker. The jetty posts were thickly populated with algae and
mussels; beyond them, the reeds rose up towards the surface.
From time to time a fish would peep from the thicket, usually
a tench or a char. Sometimes a rare pearly roach would even
put in an appearance, hovering motionless in the water for a
few seconds before disappearing into the darkness again with
a single flap of its fins. Little Franz sat quietly on the bottom,
listening to the lake. He heard the rushing of the deep water
moving to and fro, the glugging of waves on the surface, here

and there a rustle in the reeds, and sometimes, from afar, the faint thump of the ferries. He felt the soft meadow of algae under his buttocks and saw how the tiny floating particles shimmered above him in the sunbeams. Hours later, as he ran home on the path along the shore with the evening sun shining in his face, he still carried this silent green world within him and yearned for it a little.

'If you're going to take root, you'd better do it outside!'

It was an old voice, high and cracked. Directly in front of Franz, at about chest height, the head appeared to which the voice belonged. It was completely bald, and it lacked eyebrows, too, which made it look rather lizard-like in the greenish light.

'One schilling, if you want to see the show. If not, the exit's over there, right where the entrance just was!'

Only now did Franz see the box office window: a small, square opening in the wall. The lizard was sitting behind it in the half-dark, staring out at him.

'One for the show, please,' said Franz, and placed a schilling on the shelf of the counter.

The lizard took the money and held out an entry ticket. 'Unreserved seating, no interval, enjoy the programme.'

An inconspicuous door opened in the wallpaper, and Franz went through. The room beyond was much bigger than he had expected and completely red. Ceiling, lampshades, worn carpet, wallpaper — all were bathed in a soft, dark red that flickered with the shadows from innumerable candles. Behind a mirrored bar a girl was fiddling with bottles and glasses. She couldn't have been older than sixteen. She had a finger-length scar on her right cheek and the squashed nose of a boxer. There were twenty or so round tables scattered throughout the room, only a few of which were occupied — all of them by solitary men, as far as Franz could tell. The candlelight flickered over a hairy nape, a wrinkled forehead, a labourer's hand with dry clay stuck to the back, an old man's threadbare suit collar.

Franz sat at an empty table. The girl came over, and he ordered a pint of lager. She brought the beer, silently placed a bowl of nuts in front of him as well, and disappeared again behind the bar. A few minutes passed, and then suddenly a spotlight went on, illuminating a tiny wooden stage at the far end of the room. A door opened and a small man in a tuxedo stepped into the light. He was skinny and wrinkled, but despite his age he sparkled with energy. He bowed, smiling, then immediately pitched himself forward, executed a breakneck somersault, stood bolt upright again a moment later and began to speak. He talked about conditions in his beloved city of Vienna, about this great big kindergarten where the Schuschnigg boy and his playmates loved to romp about but hadn't been allowed to for ages now; about the little Nazis, who loved to scrap in the sandpit with the little Sozis, and about the little Catholics, who stood silently on the sidelines, shat their nappies, then went and confessed everything to the Greater German nannies. He spoke quickly, in a manic staccato, without even seeming to draw breath, but his smile never faltered. All at once a jolt passed through his body and he fell to his knees. With theatrical slowness he put his hands together, gazed up into the spotlight and began to pray:

Dear God, please strike me dumb,
so Dachau won't be where I'll come.
Dear God, please strike me deaf,
so I'll think we've a future left.
Dear God, please strike me blind,
so I'll believe we're doing fine.
When I'm deaf and blind and dumb,
I'll be Adolf's favourite son . . .

The men laughed, several clapped, one signalled to the wait-ress, one called after her with some well-intentioned ribaldry. Franz laughed, too, although secretly he wasn't sure he'd really understood it all properly. But it was funny, anyway, to see this little man kneeling there on the bare boards and gazing up at the ceiling, full of humility. Just like the old women with their rosaries and prayer books in front of the altar of the chapel back in Nussdorf; like crows in their black headscarves, thought Franz, popping three nuts into his mouth. Up on stage, the show continued.

The man catapulted himself back onto his feet, turned away and, with a few swift movements, adjusted his face.

When he turned round again, a murmur ran through the audience. In the cone of the spotlight, surrounded by shimmering dust, stood Adolf Hitler. A couple of strands of hair, a bit of kohl around the eyes and a square stuck onto the upper lip were enough to transform a man in a tuxedo into the German chancellor. Hitler's eyes gleamed like the dark molluscs Franz had plucked so often from the reeds and later cracked open to feed to cats or rub in girls' hair. He snapped his heels together with a sharp click, yanked his arm up in the salute and stuck out his chin. Franz couldn't help thinking of the professor, whose chin also always seemed slightly ahead of the rest of his body. Funny, he thought; perhaps he'd just identified a small thing that the two men, who were in fact otherwise very different, had in common. With an imperious gesture, Hitler called for the audience to be silent and began to give a speech. It was about the stupidity of the Orient, bravely opposed by the determination and resistance of the Aryan race; about saving Austria from the malevolence of the Balkans; about saving Europe from the voraciousness of Bolshevism; about saving the world from the insatiable greed of international Jewry, and so on. All of this had panache, and it sounded sort of reasonable, too. But as it went on he started talking himself into more and more of a frenzy, and soon the torrent of words, still comprehensible to begin with, became an inarticulate, staccato bellowing. The Chancellor of the Reich ranted and raved until spittle was flying everywhere.

He drew his head down between his shoulders, ground his jaw and bared his teeth. At the same time he doubled up, leaning his upper body forwards and bending his knees, hunching his back as he did so and balling his hands into tightly clenched fists. A glittering thread of drool dangled from his lower lip and dripped onto the boards of the stage. He let himself fall forward, braced his knees and fists against the floor and stared out into the audience with a low growl. His rear end dropped; with a guttural sound he took a deep breath and tensed his muscles to spring. Suddenly the girl with scar was standing beside him. 'Sit!' she said, in a quiet voice, and he obeyed. He laid his head between his front paws with a little whine and looked up at her. She raised her hand and for a moment it looked as if she was going to hit him, a big slap right in the middle of his stupid doggy face. But then she smiled. 'Good Adi, nice dog!' she said, and scratched him lovingly behind his ear. She pulled a lead out of the pocket of her apron, put it round his neck and, with the animal at her heel and the audience applauding, walked towards the exit. Just before they reached the door Adi jumped up, ripped the little moustache off his lip and gave the waitress a smacking kiss on the cheek. The two of them bowed, and the master of ceremonies announced the next number.

'Ladies and gentlemen — or rather, lady-less gentlemen, I am delighted to be able to present to you an international sensation of the very highest order! Beyond the heat-shimmering deserts of the New World, amid the endless expanses of the prairie, in a place where the coyote howls, the eagle circles majestically and every evening the dust from mighty herds of bison darkens the crimson of the setting sun; in a place as remote as only Hell or Paradise can be, where the salmon leap straight into the greedy mouth of the bear and the treacherous snake rattles beneath the hot stone; in just such a place we found her, naked and defenceless in the tall grass, at the mercy of the powerful forces of Nature, a lonely child of man, her quaking heart shielded in the awakening body of a young woman, the last survivor of a lost world beyond our civilization, a world in which humankind still lives in the eternal freedom of Nature, entirely in the moment, without taboos, without guilt and without shame. My dear sirs, please welcome with me tonight, right here and now: N'Djina, the shy beauty from the land of the Indians!'

The men shifted on their chairs, downed the last of their beer and licked the foam from their lips. In the meantime the girl with the scar had pushed a trolley with a huge gramophone onto the stage. The master of ceremonies put on a record and tenderly lowered the pickup. A mysterious rustling issued from the depths of the horn, and then the music began. Franz held his breath. A single nut slipped from his mouth and fell back into the bowl. He had never heard anything like it. As it squeezed the notes out, the gramophone seemed to be in pain; the rhythm was slow and thudding, the melody mournful; only occasionally did a single high note break forth. Then came the singing. It was impossible to tell whether the voice belonged to a man or a woman. It was deep, raw and broken: a murmuring, sobbing and lamentation that had strayed into this smoky Prater grotto by some strange accident and seemed to tell of some far distant world. For a moment Franz felt as if an infinitely vast space were opening up deep inside him, filled with nothing but sadness. It was strange, he thought, closing his eyes, but for some reason this infinitely vast, sadness-filled space didn't even feel that bad. Perhaps, he mused, you could let yourself fall into it, sink deeper and deeper into yourself and never come back to the surface. Just at that moment the pickup hopped across the record with a scratching sound, the voice stumbled, and Franz opened his eyes again. Directly in front of him, in the middle of the spotlight, stood the Indian woman. She was standing with her back to the audience, not moving. Her hair was pitch black and flowed in long, smooth strands over her shoulders and back. A feather was affixed to a leather headband. Her arms were naked, and she had propped her hands on her hips, where they rested on the waistband of a short, fringed, colourfully embroidered skirt. She was barefoot, and thin leather ribbons, glittering with tiny glass beads, were wound around her ankles. Her legs shone in the light. They were firm legs, smooth, rosy and plump. But it was mainly by the hollows in the backs of her knees that he recognized her. Not all that long ago he had buried his face in these hollows, had probed them, millimetre by millimetre, with his tongue, before embarking towards higher ground. These hollows were softer than anything Franz had ever known. Softer than the lake on a quiet late summer's day, softer than the moss in the little wood on Nussdorf's southern shore, softer even than his mother's hand, which in days gone by had lain so often on his cheek, in comfort, as a reward, or for no particular reason — a brief touch, as if incidental, in passing.

The voice from the gramophone gave a raw, strangled sob, and at that moment Anezka began to move. At first it was just the tapping of a foot; then her legs started to twitch, and a moment later her bottom was swaying gently up and down. She raised her arms and waved them slowly above her head. The drumbeats from the gramophone seemed to strike her body directly, another little impact with every bar. Suddenly she turned around. Her face was painted with yellow and red stripes. She was staring into the distance, her gaze lost some-where above the men's heads. Her hair completely covered her breasts. She threw her head back, laughed up at the spotlight and spread her arms wide, as if to embrace the light itself. Then she started stamping to the languid rhythm of the music. The glass beads on her feet clicked and the feather on her head bounced in time. Franz saw a single bead of sweat slip out from beneath her hairline, run down her forehead and catch on one of the pitch-black, painted eyebrows. The spectators were growing increasingly restless; one man began to slap his thighs with both hands, and there was a hoarse cough from the semi-darkness of an alcove. Anezka stamped on the wooden floor until dust swirled up in little clouds, but a moment later her body had calmed again and was gently swaying and rocking back and forth. Suddenly she grabbed her hair with both hands, parted it and let it fall back on either side over her shoulders. It was a simple movement, as casual as the opening of a curtain, but it had a tremendous effect. Some men smiled like imbeciles. Others froze. One gave a high-pitched laugh. Another fell back in his chair as if relieved of a heavy burden. Franz stared at Anezka's breasts. Just a little while ago he had lain with his face between them, had snuffled happily into this infinitely soft valley and felt strangely at home. Now her bosom was on display for all to see. Common property. A tourist attraction. The worst thing, though, was that she seemed to be enjoying it. She writhed in the light and shook her breasts as if it were only pleasant and natural. Perhaps it was. With a coquettish laugh she threw back her head again, turned round, grabbed her fringed skirt and slowly raised it. It was like the rising of the moon, greeted with murmurs or silent, staring wonder from the figures at their tables and in the safety of their dark alcoves. Franz felt his heart contract into a knot. He took his beer, pressed the cool glass to his temple, set it down again, put a bank note on the table and left the grotto without another glance at the stage.

Outside it was unexpectedly warm. Soon it would be spring.

The courtyard smelled of damp walls and refuse. Franz sat on one of the dustbins, staring up at the dirty light bulb. A little moth was fluttering madly round it. Sometimes its wings hit the socket or the wire, making an odd, papery sound. Then it touched the hot glass, and for a moment it looked as if its wings were glowing. It fell to earth like a little shadow falling from Heaven.

The grotto was slow to empty. One man after another came outside and staggered off between the wooden fences that enclosed the narrow alley, pursuing their alcohol-shrouded fantasies. No one seemed to notice Franz, not even the lizard or the girl with the scar, who left the establishment in quick succession. The last to emerge were Anezka and the master of ceremonies. He locked up, put his hand on her cheek, stroked her briefly under her eye with his thumb, and said something. She laughed quietly and lit herself a cigarette. Just then Franz leaped down from the bin. Quick as a flash the man bent over, reached under his trouser leg and pulled a thin knife from a leather sheath strapped to his calf.

'Stand still,' he said calmly, 'or I'll slit you open from belt to chin and back again!'

The blade shimmered dully in the light from the bulb. For a while there was silence in the courtyard. The only sound was a quiet rustling in one of the dustbins.

'Put it away, Heinzi,' said Anezka. 'I know him.'

The master of ceremonies hesitated for a second, then hid the knife under his trouser leg again.

'Is okay, Heinzi,' she said. 'I must to speak with him!'

He seemed to consider this for a moment. Finally he stepped right up to Franz and looked him straight in the eyes. A polished stone glittered in his left earlobe; it seemed to be lit from within by a tiny blue flame. His aftershave smelled of lavender.

'Well, I don't know you,' he said quietly. 'And it's better we never have reason to know each other. Understand?' Franz nodded. 'All right, then,' said Heinzi. He glanced quickly at Anezka, then walked away down the alley.

Anezka opened her mouth, slowly letting the cigarette smoke escape. For a few seconds her face disappeared behind a bluish veil.

'What you doing here, sonny boy?'

Franz shrugged his shoulders. 'I saw the show.'

'Was nice?'

'It was okay. Is the feather real?'

'As real as hair.'

'And him?'

'What about him?'

'Who is that?'

'Monsieur de Caballé.'

'I thought he was called Heinzi!'

'On stage called Monsieur de Caballé. Outside called Heinzi. So is showbusiness, sonny boy!'

'Aha. And what exactly does he do?'

'You see already. He do compère.'

'Compère?'

'Compère and fun and cabaret.'

'And what else?'

'What you mean, what else?'

'What does he do after the performance? More compèring and fun and cabaret — with you, perhaps?'

Anezka shrugged, briefly feeling around her mouth with her tongue before spitting a light-brown flake of tobacco onto the pavement.

'Is colleague, you understand.'

'Of course I understand!' cried Franz. 'In fact I understand very well! I saw how you two lovebirds came fluttering out of your nest!'

'Fluttering?'

'Fluttering! Anyway, one thing's quite clear: Herr de Caballé has more than just a knife in his trousers, right?'

'Some have something in trousers, some no.'

'What's that supposed to mean?'

'Ask stupid question, sonny boy, get stupid answer!'

'My name's not "sonny boy", my name's Franz!' yelled Franz, kicking a dustbin with such fury that it toppled over with a crash and rumbled across the courtyard in a wide arc, coming to a standstill only just before the wall on the opposite side.

'Get lost, Heinzi!' said Anezka, unperturbed. She was

looking at the end of the alley, where the shadow of the master of ceremonies had materialized for a moment and now slowly retreated again. Franz stared at the stinking trail of filth left by the bin.

'Do you belong to him?' he asked gloomily.

'I no belong anyone. Not even myself!'

Franz looked down at his shoes. The leather was worn and cracked, and the seams at the toes were starting to come undone. Suddenly he felt a malicious demon rising up somewhere inside him; it forced itself forward, overriding his despair.

'I'll give you five schillings if you show me your bum again!' he said. 'I bet it doesn't look bad under a light bulb, either.'

The sentence was scarcely out of his mouth before he felt like an idiot — a stupid country boy, a ridiculous tobacconist's apprentice who was already starting to fall apart at the seams.

'Sorry,' he said quietly.

'Is okay, sonny boy.' Anezka held her cigarette up to the light and followed the smoke with her eyes; it rose vertically like a trembling thread, curling into nothingness somewhere level with the gutters.

'My name's not "sonny boy",' said Franz in an empty voice. Anezka flicked her cigarette away and came and stood right in front of him. Her breath smelled of peppermint and cigarette smoke. A long, dark hair clung to the collar of her coat. She stood on tiptoe and kissed him on the forehead. Then she turned and walked off. For a while he heard her footsteps clacking down the alley, gradually fading away. On the ground, directly beneath the light bulb, lay the dead moth. Franz bent down, picked it up off the ground with the tips of his fingers, and wrapped it gently in a handkerchief.

Card with confusion of splendid roses in full bloom and three snow-white doves in the Stadtpark.

> *Dear Mama,*
> *Yesterday, for certain reasons, I couldn't bear it any more and I went to West Station for a one-way ticket to Timelkam. The woman behind the counter said two schillings please and went on varnishing her nails. And then something funny happened — this woman's attitude, the way she just couldn't care less, provoked my stubbornness. So I told her she could stick her ticket you know where and I went away again. Because I thought to myself, you can't have everyone behaving like that. And anyway, what would happen to the tobacconist's? And to Otto Trsnyek? And the professor? I have responsibilities now, don't I?*
> *Your Franz*

Card with family of ducks in foreground and Schafberg in background in rosy morning sunshine.

> *Dear Franzl,*
> *I think I'm quite familiar with your 'certain reasons'. But let me*

tell you something: today's reasons are already yesterday's tomorrow, and by the day after tomorrow, if not before, they're forgotten. If you'd suddenly appeared at the kitchen window I would probably have had a heart attack for sheer joy. Nonetheless, I'm proud of you that you didn't come. Yes, you have responsibilities! To your own conscience, above all. And you'll be coming home soon enough. Sending you a big hug and squeezing you as hard as I can,
Your Mama

'I'm a nobody. A worthless piece of muck. A doormat for humanity to wipe its feet on. A dustbin filled to the brim with bad thoughts, bad feelings and bad dreams. That's how it is. On top of which, I'm unattractive. Unsightly. Unappetizing. And fat. Oh God, I'm so fat! A great fat hippopotamus. A portly ten-ton walrus. A pathologically distended female elephant. All that'll be left of me after my death is a blob of fat the size of a lake. Oh, Herr Professor, if only I were dead already! If only it were all already over, done with, finished!'

Mrs. Buccleton started sobbing again. Her chin quivered, her cheeks shook, her whole body began to quake. She was indeed severely overweight, and no beauty in other respects, either. The only notable thing about her, aside from her corpulence, was her pale blue child-like eyes, which were usually very wide and seemed permanently ready to fill with tears at the slightest provocation. Mrs. Buccleton's hysteria was absolutely typical of the condition. She was American, extremely wealthy, forty-five years old, and came from a sunny but tedious small town in the Midwest. Spoiled by her father, who had died young, never liked by her mother, cheated and run out on by both of her husbands, she had tried to bury her lifelong anguish beneath mountains of jellied pork, pies and cherry cake. Since she had first entered the consulting room a couple of months earlier, her progress had been modest. She always arrived an upstanding woman of the world, but no sooner had she allowed herself to be helped out of her bespoke loden jacket — made by a tailor famed well beyond the city limits, who specialized in extra-large clothing — and lowered herself onto the couch, wheezing quietly from the exertion, than she turned into a helpless, snivelling little child who, in addition, made a mess of the expensive cushion covers by smearing them with tears and makeup. Strangely, Professor Freud liked her nonetheless. For some reason he suspected that beneath her irritating demeanour and the thick layer of fat there was a virile mind and an open heart. She also paid on time and in dollars.

'Go on,' he said. As always he sat at the head of the couch, watching the toe of his own shoe bobbing slightly up and down.

'And I get fatter with every passing day!' continued Mrs. Buccleton. 'I've put on a few kilos this month, too. My clothes no longer fit me. Or rather, I no longer fit into my clothes. But it's got to the point where I'm ashamed to go to the tailor. I'm ashamed to go anywhere at all. I'm ashamed to be seen by my own reflection. And above all I'm ashamed to be lying here in front of you, Herr Professor!'

Freud leaned back a little further. The only real reason why, in all of the innumerable therapy sessions over the past few decades, he had retreated behind the head of the couch was that he couldn't bear being stared at by his patients for a whole hour. Nor could he bear having to look into their faces: beseeching, angry, despairing, contorted by other emotions. Lately in particular he had often felt overwhelmed by the exhausting hours with his patients, helplessly observing their suffering, which for each and every one of them seemed to encompass the entire world. How had he ever come up with the ridiculous idea that he wanted to understand this suffering, or that he might even be able to alleviate it? What on earth had got into him to make him devote the best part of his life to illness, depression and misery? He could have remained a physiologist and gone on cutting insect brains into wafer-thin slices with his scalpel. Or written novels: exciting adventure stories set in far-off countries and ancient times. Instead, here he was, contemplating Mrs. Buccleton's round head from the shadow of the corner where he sat. Her bleached-blonde hair was grey at the roots, and as she sniffed quietly her nostrils quivered. Viewed from this angle, Mrs. Buccleton's nose looked like a pudgy little animal quaking with fear on being abandoned in an unfamiliar and threatening wilderness. There was something about it that Freud found touching. At the same time, he was annoyed at himself for being touched. It was always things like this, apparently small and trifling, that made him forget the distance he so painstakingly established between himself and his patients: the crumpled handkerchief in a director-general's hand, an old teacher's crooked wig, an undone shoelace, a quiet swallow, a couple of dropped words, or, like now. Mrs. Buccleton's trembling nose.

'So you're ashamed,' he said. 'What are you ashamed of?'

'Everything. My legs. My neck. The sweat patches under my arms. My face. My whole appearance. Even at home, even under my blankets, I'm ashamed. I'm ashamed of everything I do, have, and am.'

'Hmm,' said Freud. 'And what about pleasure?'

'Excuse me?'

'What about pleasure? Don't you feel something like pleasure, too, sometimes?'

Mrs. Buccleton considered. Outside in the courtyard someone opened a window; two women's voices were heard briefly, scolding, then all was quiet again. Freud's gaze slid across his collection of antiquities. They needed to be dusted again at some point, thoroughly, he thought. The terracotta horseman already had a thin layer of dust on his head, and he even thought he could see the delicately shimmering thread of a spider's web hanging from the Chinese watchman's left ear.

Perhaps, thought Freud, at some point his own bust would stand in some room, waiting silently for someone with a damp cloth to wipe the dust from its bald pate.

'I feel pleasure when I'm eating,' said Mrs. Buccleton. 'When I'm eating a big piece of cake, for example.'

'Oh,' said Freud, and his chin slowly dropped onto his chest.

'There you are!' cried Mrs. Buccleton.

'Where am I?'

'You despise me!'

'What makes you think that?'

'Your "Oh" had a despising undertone! Devaluating and despising! Also, you lowered your head. Did you think I didn't notice? I know the sound of your beard on your collar!'

Freud involuntarily sat up straight in his armchair and stuck out his chin. A moment later, though, he was annoyed at his own little insecurity, the ridiculous sense of having been caught in the act, like a schoolchild making faces behind the teacher's back.

'My dear Mrs. Buccleton, allow me to say the following,' he growled, with all the affability he could muster at that moment. 'My "Oh" had neither a devaluing nor a despising nor any other kind of undertone. Rather, my "Oh" was simply the expression of my attentiveness in the form of a sound. And if, from time to time, my head yields to the force of gravity, I would ask you to be so kind as to forgive it. It is now more than eighty years old, has done a lot of work in its lifetime and rests on a set of rather brittle cervical vertebrae.'

'I'm sorry, Herr Professor,' sniffed Mrs. Buccleton, in a small voice.

'To return to our subject matter, dear lady,' Freud continued sternly, 'shame and pleasure are like siblings who go through life hand in hand — if we allow them to. For reasons that are still hidden in the darkness of your past, but which, with your gracious assistance, I intend, in the foreseeable future, to bring forth into the light of understanding, only one of the siblings is thriving, while the other is wasting away and only comes into its own in confectionery shops, if at all.'

'Do you think so?'

'Yes, I think so.'

'But what can I do to help the poor thing come into its own?' asked Mrs. Buccleton hopefully.

Freud leaned forward, folded his arms across his chest, looked his patient in the eyes and gave her his most piercing stare. 'Stop eating cakes!'

With a cry of pain that rose from the very depths of her soul, Mrs. Buccleton thrashed her heavy body about until the couch legs creaked, the parquet shuddered, and the army of antiquities on the shelves began to tremble and jump as if, after centuries of paralysis, it had finally come to life.

When Mrs. Buccleton had left, the professor stood at the window a while longer looking down into the courtyard. It had grown warm over the last few days; the snow had long since melted, and the chestnut trees would soon be budding. Yesterday, Schuschnigg had made a big speech to his people. He had appeared in public in his home town of Innsbruck, wearing a traditional Tyrolean suit, and had asked his listeners whether they intended to vote for a 'free, German, independent, social, Christian and united Austria' in the plebiscite announced for the thirteenth of March. And as more than twenty thousand supporters bellowed their assent into the clear Tyrolean mountain air, Adolf Hitler was probably sitting beside the radio somewhere in Berlin, licking his lips. Austria lay before him like a steaming schnitzel on a plate. Now was the time to carve it up. After Schuschnigg's speech there were violent clashes between his supporters and opponents in Vienna. The patriots swarmed out all over the city roaring, 'Heil Schuschnigg!' and 'We're voting yes!' Now, though, backed by the power of the silent masses, the National Socialists were crawling out of their holes again, too, and running noisily through the streets. 'Heil Hitler!' they shouted. 'One people! One Reich! One Führer!' The braying of scattered riotous assemblies echoed through the streets well into the early hours of the morning, like the furious barking of dogs.

Frau Szubovic, the caretaker's gossipy wife, appeared in the courtyard, waved up at the professor and started scattering pigeon poison in corners. Freud pretended he hadn't seen her and quickly took a step back into the room. Unanswered letters were piled up on his desk. The whole world seemed to want something from him. People were cosseting their faint-hearted troubles and hadn't even noticed yet that the earth beneath their feet was burning. He picked up one of the non-descript letters and opened it. 'Esteemed Herr Professor Dr. Sigmund Freud! Next year our well-known and much-loved publishing house, Earthwork, is publishing an anthology with the provisional title *Indigenous Orchards as Places of Spiritual Contemplation*. With this in mind, Herr Professor, we are taking the liberty of requesting a short essay on the topic, or at least a few introductory words . . .' He scrunched up the letter with a weary gesture and threw it at the wastepaper basket. The ball bounced off the edge of the basket, rolled back over the parquet and landed right in front of his feet. He felt a brief urge to give it a furious kick and send it flying across the room, but just then there was a rap at the door. It was, unmistakably, his daughter Anna. Martha knocked. Anna rapped.

'What is it?' grumbled the professor.

'He's back again.'

'Who?'

'The boy from the tobacconist's.'

Freud's expression brightened. He had, in fact, always felt slightly awkward and out of place in the presence of so-called 'common people'. With this Franz, though, it was different. The boy was blossoming. And not like the knitted blossoms on one of the many blankets his wife always draped so carefully over the couch, whose thick woollen fibres seemed, in some magical way, to collect the dust of the entire city — not faded and worn out from decades of sitting. No, this young person was not only still rather naïve, he also pulsated with fresh, vigorous life. Furthermore, the colossal difference between their ages automatically established the distance that Freud found agreeable and which was, indeed, the thing that made close contact with the majority of his fellow humans tolerable in the first place. Franz was very young, whereas the professor's world was threatening to grow increasingly old. Even his daughter was already over forty, although suddenly he felt as if it were just the day before yesterday that he had perched on the edge of the bathtub brushing her milk teeth. Then there were the patients, as well as all his other relatives and the few friends who were still left. Slowly, with an old man's small steps, you tottered progressively towards petrification, until in the end, without anyone really noticing, you could take your place in your own antiquities collection.

'Papa?' Anna had entered the room, without rapping a second time. She was wearing trousers again. The professor hated women's legs in trousers, including, and especially, his daughter's. In certain matters, however, it was inadvisable to start an argument with her, so as far as he was concerned she could wear her trousers. As long as she stayed at home in them.

'Is he sitting on the bench again?'

Anna nodded. 'For the past hour and a half.'

'Has he brought something?'

'That I don't know. But you shouldn't go out any more, anyway.'

'Why not?'

'You know perfectly well.'

Freud shrugged his shoulders. Of course he knew. He was old. He was sick. He was a Jew. And there were far too many ruffians on the streets. But there could be no question of capitulating before events that hadn't even really begun yet. And certainly not of capitulating before his own daughter.

'No, I don't know,' he said, stubbornly. 'Now fetch me my coat and hat.'

Anna smiled. She stepped over to her father and took hold of his chin. He opened his mouth, and she pushed her thumb carefully into his jaw. With the tip she pressed firmly on the back of the prosthesis. There was a click, and he grimaced in pain.

'In place,' said Anna, after glancing briefly into his oral cavity. She withdrew her thumb, wiped it with a handkerchief, stood on her toes and kissed her father quickly on both cheeks.

'Yes, all right,' he murmured, stepping back and rubbing his beard. Over the decades he had learned to cope with pain; perhaps one day he would succeed in doing the same with expressions of affection.

'Look after yourself,' said Anna. Then she bent down, picked up the orchard owner's crumpled letter and dispatched it, with a well-aimed throw, into the wastepaper basket.

Just as Franz was preparing himself for a long wait and, contrary to all the time-honoured rules of Viennese decorum, putting his feet up to stretch out the whole length of the bench, the door across the road opened and the professor stepped outside. Like the first time, he crossed the road with steps that, though shaky, were nonetheless fairly assertive, and headed straight for the bench.

'Did it ever occur to you to ring the bell?' he asked. 'It would make things a lot easier.'

'It did occur to me,' answered Franz, who had immediately leaped to his feet and hurried towards Freud. 'I just didn't dare disturb you.'

'Sometimes you have to disturb people if you want to reach them!' said Freud. He handed Franz a little parcel, carefully wrapped in tissue paper. 'Here's your scarf back. It's been washed and ironed and smells like a rosebush. The ladies have given it their all.'

'Please send my heartfelt thanks and very esteemed greetings up to the first floor, Herr Professor! But don't you want to sit down?' said Franz, with an inviting sweep of his hand.

'No thank you,' said Freud, casting a furtive glance at the first-floor living-room window, which reflected the clear spring sky. 'Today we're going for a walk.'

They walked up Berggasse, turned left on Währingerstrasse, walked in an arc around the Votive Church and on towards the Town Hall. The air was mild; it hadn't snowed for weeks, and the lilac was in bloom in the Votive Park, far too early. A gentle *foehn* wind had swept in from the mountains and was blowing a tremendous number of flyers about the streets, encouraging people to vote that Sunday. YES TO AUSTRIA, they read, and RED-WHITE-RED UNTIL WE'RE DEAD! Franz had slipped the parcel with the scarf beneath his shirt, where it warmed his belly, crackling quietly. So the ladies had given it their all, he thought, and tried not to carry his pride before him like a lantern. He kept glancing out of the corner of his eye at the professor, who was walking alongside him, taking small steps. His cane clacked on the pavement in a steady rhythm, as if he first had to feel his way; he breathed shallowly and irregularly as he did so, with a quiet hissing sound on every exhalation. It made Franz want to giggle. Or actually laugh out loud. He had, in fact, always felt a bit clumsy and out of his element around so-called 'clever people'. But with the professor it was different. This old man wasn't just clever. Back at the lake you were considered well-read if you could more or less decipher the headlines on the parish newsletter or the timetable at Timelkam Station. And after a few pints of beer in the Goldener Leopold, if not before, all the doctors and high school teachers from Vienna, Munich or Salzburg who came in droves in summer to lie on the shore, burning their white fish-bellies pink, proved that, when it came down to it, they were really quite ordinary minds, not to mention tellers of very dull stories. The professor, though, was so clever that if he wanted to read a book he could just go and write it himself. That's how it is, thought Franz, and smiled, as they walked on in the shadow of the long university building. But there was something else as well. A single thought, which popped abruptly into his mind like a tiny shock and quickly spread, deep within him, to become a persistent feeling: a feeling that had now claimed a place for itself and — this much was clear — would not easily be banished again. He felt sorry for the professor. There were many things about him that touched Franz somehow. The lopsided jaw, for example. Or his back, which was always slightly bent. The narrow, square shoulders. The old fingers, withered and blotchy, that clung to the knob of his walking stick. Getting old is a wretched business, thought Franz. He felt melancholy and, at the same time, rather angry. What was the point of all that cleverness if Time got you in the end anyway?

In front of the town hall, children and youths were gathered in small groups. They were hanging around on corners, standing arm in arm, blocking the pavements or running across the square, laughing and shouting, waving hats and swastika flags. A few solitary policemen stood watching the goings-on with their hands behind their backs. A boy of primary school age in short trousers crowed '*Sieg Heil!*' and flung himself backwards onto the grass, arms and legs outstretched. The Friday afternoon traffic roared down Ringstrasse. Engines puttered, horses' hooves clattered on the cobbles, coachmen clicked their tongues and flicked their thin whips hissing through the air.

The pavements were populated with people chattering and talking over each other. It was warm, the sun was shining, there was a pleasant breeze. People were preparing for the weekend, for the next step, for the future; things were happening in the city, in the country, out in the world. A diesel truck lumbered slowly past with a group of labourers on the back. The men waved their hats and chanted slogans against Hitler and for the Austrian working classes. One of the men leaped from the moving vehicle after his flat cap; he had thrown it up high in the air and it had been carried away by the wind. He landed awkwardly, fell over and lay motionless on his side. A little crowd immediately formed around him. The truck drove on.

Franz and the professor passed the Burgtheater on their left and went into the Volksgarten. Here too the lilac was blooming all around. The tall hedges and trees muffled the noise from the road, and the earth, thickly overgrown with grass, exuded a cool dankness. Franz had never been here before. He would have liked to walk a bit and look around, and he would have liked even more to creep secretly under one of the bushes with the professor and discuss all manner of things in the leafy green twilight, undisturbed. Freud, however, headed purposefully for the other end of the park, where they found an empty bench in an alcove in the hedge beneath an old chestnut tree, and sat down. Franz reached carefully into his breast pocket and took out a beautiful Hoyo de Monterrey. Freud accepted the cigar, holding it up in front of his face and contemplating its silhouette for a while before sticking it in his mouth and lighting it. During their walk neither of them had said a word, and now too they sat beside each other in silence. The professor puffed little clouds of smoke into the air, his jaw creaking. Someone a long way off yelled, 'Heil Hitler!' There was a cheer. High-pitched laughter. Then the muffled sound of traffic again.

Suppressing a groan, the professor leaned back and squinted up for a while at the flurry of leaves pierced by flashes of sunlight. Finally he said, 'Our meetings must be costing you quite a bit.'

'Excuse me, Herr Professor?'

'A cigar of this quality is not exactly inexpensive.'

'But it's harvested by brave men on the fertile banks of the San Juan y Martínez River and tenderly hand-rolled by beautiful women,' said Franz, nodding earnestly.

'Although it is not entirely clear to me in this context why bravery, of all things, should be such an outstanding characteristic of the Cuban tobacco farmer,' Freud replied. 'But that's just by the by. If, on the other hand, we're talking about beautiful women, I hope your endeavours with regard to the female sex have met with success. Whatever form this success may have taken.'

'That's exactly why I wanted to speak with you,' said Franz bitterly. 'My endeavours have met with nothing whatsoever. Although, on the other hand, I'm not at all sure about that. I just don't know. Basically, I don't know anything at all.'

'That realization is, at least, the first step up the steep stairs towards wisdom,' Freud replied. 'But first let's try to shine a little light into the obscurity. Did you look for her?'

'Yes, Herr Professor.'

'Did you find her?'

'Yes, Herr Professor.'

'Did you ask her what she was called?'

'Yes, Herr Professor.'

'Am I supposed to squeeze the words from your cerebral cortex one by one?'

'No, Herr Professor. She's called Anezka.'

'Bohemian?'

'Yes. From a beautiful village called Dobrovice, curled up to the hill Viničný as if to a dark lover, in the district of Mladá Boleslav.'

'A hill like a dark lover?'

Franz nodded sadly. Freud fished a match out of its box, lit it, and held it carefully to the glowing surface, which was threatening to become a little uneven.

'Bohemian cuisine is really quite wonderful,' he said, dreamily contemplating his Hoyo, which now burned steadily again.

'Yes, wonderful,' murmured Franz. Across from them, on the other side of a still bare and wintry rose bed, two weather beaten ladies walked past giving pointed looks at the two men so casually occupying the bench that was in fact, by right of custom, theirs. A park attendant came sauntering up from the opposite direction. He greeted them by briefly raising a hand to the peak of his cap, and began to poke about with a thin stick in the rubbish bin beside the bench.

The gentlemen must please excuse him, he said as he did so; it's because of the bombs. And of course, he added, because of all the other items the municipality found unacceptable.

What items would those be, exactly, Freud wanted to know.

The park attendant shrugged. Impossible to say, he replied; you'd probably only find out if you found such an item.

Why did people think they might find suspicious items and bombs in the rubbish bins in the Volksgarten, of all places, Freud asked.

Why not, argued the park attendant, why not there, of all places, or even especially: in the Volksgarten rubbish bins? After all, you couldn't read a bomber's mind. But they'd have to excuse him; the Volksgarten wasn't small, after all, and rubbish bins in Vienna were like grains of sand on the shore. Have a nice day, gentlemen, goodbye.

'Right,' said Freud, once the attendant had disappeared behind the hedge. 'So what exactly happened with you and this Anezka?'

'I touched her,' said Franz. 'And it was the most beautiful experience I've ever had in my life.'

'I'm glad to hear it. I hope she touched you, as well?'

'Of course! And how! Everywhere! And every spot where she touched me is still burning. My whole body is burning like a match!'

Freud tapped his cigar thoughtfully with his middle finger. 'Love is a wildfire that no one wants to or is able to extinguish,' he said, observing the flakes of ash spinning slowly down towards the gravel.

'I do!' cried Franz, leaping up impetuously from the bench. 'I'm able to and I want to extinguish it! I don't want to end up a little pile of ashes in the back room of a tobacconist's shop!'

'Sit down and stop shouting in public,' Freud commanded, with sudden sharpness. Franz obeyed. 'Now then: once more, slowly and calmly. So you've seen her again. You know what she's called. You know where she's from. You touched each other. What else?'

'Then she disappeared.'

'Again?'

'That's the point: she was just gone! Not even the women in the yellow house could tell me where she was.'

'The women in the yellow house?'

'All Bohemians. Except the old woman with her pig.'

The professor raised his eyes to the heavens as if anticipating some form of practical encouragement to descend from that radiant blue. But nothing came. He took off his hat with a weary gesture and placed it on one of his knees.

'If the pig has no appreciable significance for the ongoing development of the story, I would ask that you carry on and finish it before the world comes to an end, which, as we know, could happen at any moment!'

'Sorry, Herr Professor,' said Franz contritely. 'So she disappeared. But after a couple of weeks I found her again. I sat down behind a rubbish heap in front of the yellow house and lay in wait for her. Then I followed her. To the Prater. Into the grotto. The grotto is a cabaret. Or a dance club. Or both. In any case: green outside, red inside, smoky, stuffy, lots of candles and so forth. I ordered something to drink, and first of all Monsieur de Caballé came on.'

'Who?'

'His real name is Heinzi. He tells jokes and makes Hitler into a dog. The waitress led him away on a lead, and the music started.'

'What sort of music?'

'Don't know. Quite rhythmical; sort of sad, as well. Anyway, then Anezka came on.'

'Finally.'

'Yes. But it wasn't actually Anezka at all, it was an Indian girl called N'Djina. Or rather, it was Anezka, of course, but in an Indian costume, with a wig and feathers and all the bits and bobs. And she danced. It wasn't a normal dance, though. It was quite an . . . exciting dance.'

'Could you perhaps express yourself more precisely?'

'She took off her clothes. She bared her stomach, her bosom and her bottom to the spotlight.'

'And I'm guessing that this was the most beautiful thing you'd ever seen in your life?'

'Yes, it was. Although I'd seen it all already. Only the terrible thing about it was that this time a load of other men were there, too! Anyway, I left, and sat down on a dustbin outside the entrance. Later on she came out as well. Not on her own, though. Monsieur de Caballé was with her.'

'Heinzi?'

'Yes. He pulled a knife from his trousers, but then he calmed down again and left me alone. We talked, Anezka and I, and while we were talking she looked at me so coldly. I hated her for it. At the same time, I felt sorry for her. Because she has to bare her bottom to the light in front of these men. I felt much sorrier for myself, though. And so I kicked the dustbin and insulted Anezka, and she gave me a kiss and walked off, and a moth fell out of the sky and it was all, all, all over.'

The professor closed his eyes and drew deeply on the Hoyo. With his other hand he grasped his chin and cautiously shifted his lower jaw from side to side against the pressure of his fingers. Suddenly he dropped the hand into his lap and turned his head towards Franz.

'Do you love her?'

'Excuse me, Herr Professor?'

'Do you love this Bohemian Prater girl?'

'Ha!' Franz gave a high-pitched laugh and slapped his thigh with his hand. And again, immediately afterwards: 'Ha!' Of course I do! he wanted to say. That goes without saying! he wanted to shout in the professor's face, to yell it out into the Volksgarten, into the whole world, with all the sudden, almost disturbing hilarity welling up inside him. What sort of question was that? What sort of unnecessary, idiotic, far-fetched, utterly damn fool question was that meant to be? Of course he loved her! It went without saying that he loved her! He loved, loved, loved her! More than anything else in the world! More even than his own heart and his own blood and his own life! Something like that, and much more, was what Franz wanted to shout at the professor. But, curiously, none of this came out. Not a word. Not a syllable. Instead, he remained silent. And another laugh, which had been tickling in his throat just a moment ago, had simply got stuck and was now slowly dissolving, like one of those yellow sherbet sweets that old Frau Seidlmeier in the tiny grocery shop in Nussdorf would sometimes slip to the children: they fizzed so agreeably in the mouth at first, but soon left nothing but sticky lumps on the teeth and a bitter aftertaste. Franz bowed his head.

'I don't know,' he said quietly. 'I was quite certain, actually. But now I don't know any more.'

Freud nodded slowly. Again Franz noticed how frail he was. A small, angular skull that seemed to balance on the thin neck only by a miracle. A few flecks of ash had got caught in his beard. Franz would have liked to bend forward and pluck them out, one after another.

'All right, then,' said Freud. 'I suggest that, to begin with, we clarify the terminology. I suspect that when we talk about your love, what we really mean is your libido.'

'My what?'

'Your libido. This is the force that drives people after a certain age. It causes as much joy as it does pain, and to put it in simple terms, with men, it is located in their trousers.'

'With you, too?'

'My libido was conquered long ago,' sighed the professor.

There was a sudden rustle beside the bench. A moment later a little bird came fluttering out of the hedge and landed on the gravel right in front of the men's feet. It had a body like a sparrow's but its plumage looked as if it had been bleached, with just a few pale, yellowish flecks on the side. Its eyes were red. The bird sat there for a while without moving; then it spread its wings, dipped down and began to wallow in the gravel, waggling its tail and shaking its feathers as it did so. Just as suddenly as it had started, it stopped again. It hopped twice towards the bench, froze for a moment, then finally flew up in a wide arc and away towards the ring road.

'Now even the sparrows have gone mad,' said Franz, raking his foot over the gravel.

'That was the plague bird,' murmured Freud. 'They say it only ever appears before the outbreak of disease, war and other disasters.' The cigar crackled in his hand. A slight wind had risen and was whispering in the treetops.

'Is there going to be a disaster, then, Herr Professor?'

'Yes,' said Freud, staring after the plague bird, which had long since vanished behind the Burgtheater.

'Herr Professor, I think I'm a colossal idiot,' said Franz, after a few moments of intent and thoughtful silence. 'A sheep-brained Upper Austrian imbecile from top to toe.'

'Congratulations. Insight is the midwife of recovery.'

'I just asked myself, you see, what justification there is for my stupid little worries, with all the crazy events happening in the world.'

'I think I can reassure you there. Firstly, where women are concerned, worries are usually stupid, but seldom little. Secondly, we could turn the question on its head: what justification is there for all these crazy world events, when you have your worries?'

'You're laughing at me, Herr Professor.'

'No, I am not,' Freud contradicted him, raising his cigar instead of a forefinger for emphasis. 'Current world events are nothing but a tumour, an ulcer, a suppurating, stinking bubo that will soon burst and spill its disgusting contents over the whole of Western civilization. Admittedly that's a rather drastic and graphic formulation, but it is nonetheless the truth, my young friend.'

Franz felt a peculiar pride well up in him, burst like a bubble somewhere behind his forehead and trickle down inside his head like a warm shower. He was now the professor's 'young friend'.

'The truth . . .' he repeated, nodding his head thoughtfully. 'Do people lie on your couch to hear truths like this?'

'Oh, come on,' said Freud, staring moodily at the remains of his Hoyo. 'If one only ever spoke the truth, the consultations would be as dry and empty as little deserts. Truth has a smaller part to play than people think. That's the case in life as well as analysis. Patients talk about whatever comes to mind, and I listen. Or sometimes it's the other way round: I talk about whatever comes to mind, and the patients listen. We talk and are silent and are silent and talk and, quite incidentally, explore the dark side of the soul together.'

'And how do you go about that?'

'We painstakingly grope through the darkness so that at least here and there we may bump into something useful.'

'And people have to lie down for that?'

'You could do it standing up as well, but it's more comfortable lying down.'

'I understand,' said Franz. 'That sort of reminds me of when I was younger. Sometimes, in summer, I used to creep out of the cottage in the middle of the night and go into the forest with a couple of friends. Each of us had a candle, and the trees would flicker like giant ghosts. We'd stumble around like that for a while in the dark; but we never actually came across anything really interesting. Sometimes one of us would tread on a slug. But that was about it, and then we'd go home again . . . Yes, that's what it was like,' he added, after a brief pause. 'It was a different time. Back then, it was just trees we were frightened of. So what do you and your patients encounter in the dark, Herr Professor?'

'Dreams, ideally,' said Freud. He laid the stump of the cigar beside him on the arm of the bench and watched it glow one last time before it went out for good. Carefully he picked up the little carcass and threw it into the rubbish bin where the park attendant had been poking about.

'But what about me?' cried Franz. 'I can't spend the rest of my life stumbling about in some sort of darkness, treading on slugs or dreams. It's easy for you to talk — you conquered the libido long ago. I still have to wrestle with it! My trousers are about to burst, and I don't know what to do. I don't know if I should see Anezka again. I don't know if I *want* to see her again. I don't even know if I *can* see her again. I don't know, I don't know, I don't know!'

He had jumped to his feet again and covered the distance between the rosebed and the bench several times. 'Hang it all, what on earth am I supposed to do?' he asked finally, in a weary voice, and dropped back onto the bench again. 'Help me, Herr Professor!'

Freud held up his hands, regarded them for a moment in the sunlight, and let fall them into his lap.

'I don't believe I can help you there,' he said. 'Finding the right woman is one of the most difficult tasks we face in our civilization. And each of us has to deal with it entirely alone.

We come alone into the world, and we die alone. But birth and death seem almost like great social events compared to the loneliness we feel when first we stand before a beautiful woman. In the things that matter, we have to fend for ourselves from the very beginning. We must keep asking ourselves what we want and where we want to go. To put it another way: you have to rack your own brains. And if you don't get an answer from them, ask your heart.'

'I can't expect much from my brains,' murmured Franz. 'And my heart is lying in pieces in a house in Rotensterngasse.'

'You'll find you have no alternative. If you keep asking old men for advice, you'll keep getting unsatisfactory answers. And if you ask the contents of your trousers, the answer will be unequivocal, but it will lead to nothing but confusion.'

'Hmm,' said Franz. He put one hand to his brow to try to contain the wild turmoil of his thoughts. 'Might it be, perhaps, that what your couch method does is force people to abandon their worn-out but comfortable paths and send them off across a completely unfamiliar field full of stones, where they have to struggle to find their path without the faintest idea what it looks like, how long it is, and whether it leads to any sort of destination?'

Freud raised his eyebrows and slowly opened his mouth.

'Might that be?' repeated Franz. Freud swallowed. 'Why are you looking at me so oddly, Herr Professor?'

'How am I looking at you?'

'I don't know. As if I'd just said something unbelievably stupid.'

'No, you didn't do that. You most certainly did not do that.'

Freud attempted a smile, then ran his fingers distractedly through his hair, took his hat from his knee, put it on his head and rose from the bench. 'I think we've talked enough for today. The sun will be going down soon. And who knows whether it will ever come up again.'

With remarkably quick steps, his walking stick beating time on the gravel, the professor walked back in the direction of Ringstrasse. Franz remained seated for a while. Only when the grey hat had finally disappeared behind the hedge did he jump up and run after it.

They said goodbye in Berggasse with a brief handshake. Freud's fingers felt dry and light. Like fishbones, thought Franz. Like the bones of a worm-infested carp that has ended up with the cats instead of on the restaurant customers' plates, and whose skeleton crumbles in your hands when you pulled it out a couple of weeks later from under the damaged fishing boats.

After the professor had disappeared into the house, Franz put his ear to the door and closed his eyes. The wood was still warm from the sun, and Freud's steps echoed inside in the stairwell. When Franz opened his eyes again and moved away from the door, his first steps were still rather hesitant and careful. Soon, though, he marched off decisively to the little restaurant round the corner in Türkengasse — for a goulash and a glass of beer.

The following evening Red Egon sat bent over his radio in his basement apartment in Schwarzspanierstrasse, listening to Kurt Schuschnigg's voice bereft of strength and resistance. It was the chancellor's last speech to a people that had long since ceased to be his. Coerced by Hitler's vehement threats of violence, he cancelled the plebiscite for a free Austria and announced his resignation. In order not to provoke a bloodbath when the German troops crossed the border, as it now seemed almost certain they would, he had ordered the Austrian army to offer no resistance. He closed his address with the words: 'And so, in this hour, I take leave of the Austrian people with a word of farewell uttered from the bottom of my heart: God protect Austria!' Scarcely had he finished his speech than uncontrollable roars erupted on the streets: 'One people! One Reich! One Führer!', 'Death to Judaism!', or merely inarticulate yelling, singing and howling. Red Egon switched off the radio. Through the little dust-fogged window that looked out directly onto the pavement he saw the legs of agitated Viennese men and women hurrying, running, racing past. He stood and went over to his wardrobe. For a moment he contemplated his gaunt figure, reflected in the dark glass of the door. He adjusted the knot of his tie, licked the tip of his index finger and smoothed his left eyebrow. Then he opened the wardrobe, took out a length of material rolled up in a big ball, a hammer and a few nails, and left his apartment without locking it. On the staircase he met the two sons of the railway worker couple from the second floor. Their short trousers flapped below their knees as they dashed out into the street, uttering piercing cries. Somewhat out of breath, Red Egon climbed the stairs to the top floor and entered the attic through a low door, where his toe encountered a pigeon's lifeless body. Suppressing a slight feeling of revulsion he clambered up a wooden ladder, through a skylight and onto the roof. A dusty squall hit him full in the face and he had to close his eyes for a moment. The noise from the road billowed up to him, muted: the individual voices of ten thousand Viennese citizens united in a single note that kept swelling and subsiding, a kind of wail, like a siren, to which the whole city seemed to vibrate. He walked cautiously across to the edge of the gently sloping roof and sat down. With a few blows of the hammer he fixed one end of the length of material to the tarred roof cladding. Then he simply let it roll over the guttering and heard, with satisfaction, the five metres of fabric smack against the side of the house underneath him and against the attic window of the recently deceased Frau Hinterberger. Carefully he stuck the hammer and the rest of the nails in the inside pocket of his jacket, shuffled a little further forward, swung his legs over the edge of the roof and dangled them above the roar of Schwarzspanierstrasse. The smell of roast meat reached him from an open window on the opposite side of the road. Two pigeons were perched on a chimney. From time to time one of them would draw itself up and tiptoe briefly round in a circle, the wind puffing its plumage into a fluffy ball of feathers. Red Egon slipped a crumpled packet of filterless cigarettes from his trouser pocket, took one out, placed it on his open palm and contemplated it for a while. Then he put it in his mouth and lit it. He inhaled deeply with his eyes closed. When, after precisely seven drags, the skylight flew open and three men and a woman with swastika armbands, cudgels, and faces twisted with murderous intent came crawling onto the roof, he didn't even turn round. He shifted his weight forward, flicked the cigarette into the abyss, and plunged after it.

'Have you read this?' asked Otto Trsnyek darkly, waving the morning edition of the *Reichspost* above his head. Franz shook his head. In the past few days he'd hardly got round to reading the papers, or rather had not made much effort to do so. Recent events were buzzing around in his head like a swarm of disturbed flies, and he could scarcely open a newspaper before the letters began to lift off the paper and disintegrate into an incomprehensible muddle.

'Sit down and listen, then,' the tobacconist ordered. Franz interrupted his work, which consisted of clearing the previous day's newspapers from the shelves and replacing them with new ones that smelled of fresh printer's ink. He quickly stuffed the latest issue of the *Bauernbündler* into the appropriate rack — like almost all the newspapers that week it had on its front page a photograph of Adolf Hitler looking impressive — and settled himself on his stool. The tobacconist spread the *Reichspost* out in front of him and began to read.

'"Cowardly attack thwarted! Yesterday it emerged that several Viennese men and women succeeded, through courageous intervention, in thwarting a perfidious attack on the new intellectual freedom of our Reich . . ."'

'Ha!' cried Otto Trsnyek, slapping his palm down on the sales counter. 'Did you hear that? "New intellectual freedom"!' He raised his arm again to slam his hand down on the desk but controlled himself at the last minute and continued, hoarsely: '"In the early evening, the unemployed Bolshevist Hubert Panstingl, known — indeed, notorious — in certain circles as 'Red Egon', gained access to the roof of the tenement building in which he lived on the Schwarzspanierstrasse. There he was able to proceed undisturbed and put his plan into action. He unfurled what was clearly a home-made banner; the graffiti he scrawled on it, which cannot be reproduced here, was intended to vilify our Reich, our people and our hope-filled city in a most despicable manner."'

Otto Trsnyek snatched up the paper, hopped out from behind the counter with surprising agility, bent over Franz and bellowed, 'What, may I ask, is still "hope-filled" about a city that publishes such lies — the clumsy scribblings of a filthy, jingoistic, über-Germanic tabloid?'

Franz tried to make himself as small as possible. 'Listen to what it says next!' the tobacconist cried. '"It was only thanks to the bravery of a few passersby and residents who hurried to the scene that this dangerous crank did not succeed in attacking the Viennese citizenry for any longer than necessary. Fully aware of the great danger they were putting themselves in, the men and women climbed onto the roof, confronted the deranged attacker and requested that he immediately hand over the aforementioned banner. However, the cowardly Communist Panstingl had no intention of abandoning his project; instead, he planted himself defiantly in front of these ordinary people and threatened them. We were not able to clarify before going to press whether or not a gun was involved, but statements by the parties concerned suggest that it can be assumed with relative certainty."'

'Ha!' Otto Trsnyek shouted again. 'A gun! Red Egon would rather butter his bread with his fingers than touch a knife!' By now his face was purple and dripping with sweat. He wiped his forehead with the frayed sleeves of his woolly cardigan and read on: '"However, in the course of his brutal attack it seems that the perpetrator lost his balance, tripped over the edge and fell off the roof. Fortunately no one was injured when he hit the pavement. The perpetrator is dead, and the disgraceful banner secured and destroyed."'

The tobacconist stood for a moment, swaying slightly, staring at the newspaper in his hands. Suddenly a shudder passed through his body. With quick, sharp movements he ripped the pages into smaller and smaller pieces that spun down around him to the floor. When he had finished he slowly lowered his hands. His cardigan had slipped and hung crookedly from his shoulders. The slight movement of his leg made his shoe creak quietly.

'Do you know what was written on the banner?' he whispered. Franz shook his head silently. '"Freedom of the people requires freedom of the heart. Long live freedom! Long live our people! Long live Austria!"'

Otto Trsnyek's shoe had stopped creaking. He stood quite still. A moment later he shook off his paralysis, hopped back behind the sales counter and sat down. Franz watched as he leaned back and his face slowly disappeared in the shadow behind the lamp.

That night, too, Franz had difficulty falling asleep. As always, of late. Ever since his arrival in Vienna, and despite the exhaustion that overcame him every evening, Franz found it hard to summon the sweet sleep that had always enfolded him and carried him away so easily in his bed beside the lake. Here he lay again, on his back, hands folded behind his head and eyes open, listening out into the darkness. Outside, the now customary daytime howling had metamorphosed into nocturnal whimpering, which was also now the custom. It seemed to move perpetually through the streets, and even drifted in to him in his little room at the tobacconist's. From time to time there was a gurgling in the walls. Sometimes a quiet rustling reached him from the shop. Mice, perhaps, thought Franz, or rats. Or the events of the previous day, already turned into memories and rustling out of the newspapers. It's pretty odd, actually, he thought, the way the newspapers trumpet all their truths in big fat letters only to write them small again in the next edition, or contradict them. The morning edition's truth is practically the evening edition's lie; though as far as memory's concerned it doesn't really make much difference. Because it's not usually the truth that people remember; it's just whatever's yelled loudly enough or printed big enough. And eventually, thought Franz, when one of these rustlings of memory has lasted long enough, it becomes history. He kicked off the blanket and stretched his arms in front of him. He heard his heart beating out of the mattress, indistinct, thumping quietly, like a ship's engine. That sounds nice, he thought, and he watched as his body slowly peeled away from the bed. It felt good, but it was only a brief flight. Someone shouted something after him, and far below steamers panted across the lake. The fish were showing their bellies, and a black hat rocked gently on the waves. The little flag on the horizon really couldn't be overlooked any longer. 'Excuse me, but your mother is waving!'

Franz's heart thumped him awake again, a regular pumping, getting louder. By now he had trained himself, with reasonable success, to write down his dreams. Night after night he would grope for his matches and scribble a few muddled words in the flickering candlelight on one of the pieces of squared paper he had stowed under the bed. It was a laborious process, and to begin with it made no difference. He was only really doing it for the professor's sake, and because he secretly felt guilty if he didn't. On the other hand, a degree of habit had established itself, especially over the past few days. Or a kind of satisfaction in his ability to make himself stick at it. Or perhaps even something like a small sense of relief and gratification. Franz couldn't say what it was exactly, but ultimately it didn't matter. He would write his dreams down, and afterwards — this being the rewarding side effect of all that effort — he was able to sleep peacefully for the next few hours, because he didn't dream.

A flight over the Attersee, wrote Franz in his childish scrawl, *Someone is shouting after me, the steamers are pretty, the fish aren't. The professor seems to have lost his hat, and Mother is waving at me from somewhere far away.* He put the paper and pencil under the bed and blew out the candle. For a few moments it continued to flicker behind his eyelids. Aha, he thought, it seems there's a memory flicker, too, as well as a memory rustle. He couldn't help giggling a little. Since he had left the Salzkammergut his brain kept coming up with ideas he would never have thought he had in him. Most of them were probably absolute nonsense. But still kind of interesting. He turned on his side, closed his eyes and tried to recover that sense of drifting away.

Almost exactly three seconds later he was sitting bolt

upright in bed, holding his breath. He had been jolted back to reality by a loud noise, a crashing and splintering that seemed to rip the night apart. Then silence again. Franz leaped up and ran out into the shop. Before him in the pale early morning light was a scene of unbelievable chaos. The window had been smashed, the door hung crooked on its hinges, and there were long splinters jutting from the doorframe. The floor was covered in fragments of glass; two newspaper racks had fallen over and lay piled across each other; newspapers, cigar boxes, tobacco tins, open jars of pencils and individual cigarettes were scattered all around. Outside, loose pages of newspaper were billowing on the pavement and wandering over to the other side of the road like quietly rustling ghosts. Franz took a tentative step. The glass crunched beneath his leather slippers, which the tobacconist had let him have a while ago in exchange for eight hours of unpaid overtime. A thick liquid was dripping from the doorframe and collecting in a shining puddle on the floor. And then he saw the thing on the sales counter. A black thing, a dark form, a wet heap splayed across the counter. For a moment it seemed to him to be breathing, very slowly rising and falling and rising again. It gave off an unpleasant smell: rancid, sweet, yet also slightly sour. It was the smell of old meat, of blood and shit. Cautiously, he leaned in closer. The breaths were a figment of his imagination, of course. On the counter lay the innards of one or more large animals. Flaccid scraps of tissue, gleaming lumps of fat and swollen intestines crisscrossed with fine veins. Franz stepped back and something cracked underfoot. A severed chicken head lay amid the glass splinters, looking up at him with bluish, dead eyes.

When Otto Trsnyek came to open his shop at six o'clock sharp, he didn't say a word. He surveyed the scene in silence: the crooked inscription crudely daubed above the door — JEWS SHOP HERE! — the bucketfuls of filth strewn about, the shards of glass, the blood, the chicken's heads, the stinking pile of entrails on the counter, and his apprentice Franz, who sat slumped on the stool in the windowless display, staring out at the pavement. For a long time he just stood there, speechless, without moving. Finally he opened his mouth to say something, but all that came out was a small sound, scarcely bigger than a bubble of saliva popping. And so he set to work.

Together they swept the glass up off the floor and stuffed the innards and the chicken's heads into big linen sacks that quickly became saturated with blood. They scrubbed the pavement, the walls, the tiles and shelves, and packed the dirty, soft, broken or crumbled cigars and cigarettes into a box and dumped them in a heap beside a small group of dustbins in the back courtyard. After that they carefully removed the remaining shards from the shop window frame, took the door off its hinges, hammered them straight again, put the door back on its hinges, and scrubbed the floorboards, shelves and counter a second time with vinegar and a pink, poisonous-smelling powder. A few hours later, when they had finished cleaning, the tobacconist braced both crutches against the ground, carefully placed the stump of his leg on the handles and took a deep breath. 'We'll go to the glazier later,' he said. 'First, go and fetch us a couple of beers!'

They drank the beer from the bottle, without speaking, slowly and in small gulps, the tobacconist at his post behind the counter, Franz on his stool. It was a Styrian beer, dark and bitter. It was now afternoon, and passers-by were rushing along the street; only a few paid any attention to the tobacconist's and hardly anyone stopped to glance in at the interior through the windowless shop front. Once, an emaciated dog paused and sniffed around the entrance, but its master quickly put on its lead and dragged it away. On the other side of the road Frau Dr. Dr. Heinzl hurried past. She seemed to be concentrating very hard on where she was going; at any rate, she didn't look at the tobacconist's. An elderly policeman stuck his head through the door, looked around briefly, touched his cap in salutation and disappeared again without saying a word. Somewhere behind the Wienerwald the sun began to go down; the beers had been drunk, and Otto Trsnyek cleared his throat and started to put a few words together. 'Interesting,' he said, 'that one can talk so little for a whole day.'

At that moment an old-fashioned, dark-coloured car stopped outside the entrance, and three men in grey suits got

out. One of them, a rather mournful-looking man with a yellowish, official face, knocked unnecessarily on the open doorframe. 'Herr Trsnyek?'

'We're just closing,' said the tobacconist.

The man twisted his mouth into a crooked smile. His right
ear glowed pink in the evening light. 'That may be true,' he
said, 'but only when we say so!'

'Get out of here, you swine,' hissed Otto Trsnyek quietly.
It sounded as if he were trying to spit the three men's hats off
their heads. The mournful one froze for a second, then nodded to his colleagues and stepped aside. One of the men came
through the door; the other stepped right in through the shop
window. Without seeming to draw back his arm he punched his
fist into Franz's left ear. Franz felt the warm blood spurt out of
it before he had even slid off the stool. Through the rushing
in his ear he heard the tobacconist's screams and his woollen
cardigan ripping as they grabbed him, dragged him across the
counter and flung him to the ground.

'Otto Trsnyek, I am arresting you for the possession and
distribution of pornographic material!' the mournful man cried.
There was a brief silence. Although the tobacconist was kneeling on the floor with his head bowed, Franz thought he could
make out a dark patch on his forehead.

'So where've you hidden the wank mags?' asked the mournful man. Otto Trsnyek bowed his head lower still. One of the
men kicked him hard in the ribs. He fell sideways with a grunt,

put his hands protectively in front of his face and pulled his leg in as close to his body as possible. At a nod from his boss, the third man walked behind the counter, yanked the drawer open, took out the flimsy pile of erotic magazines and held them aloft with a triumphant grin.

'You sell this kind of trash to the Jews?'

Otto Trsnyek jerked his head and opened his mouth in a barely audible 'Yes.'

'How long's this been going on?'

'Don't know.'

The mournful man nodded, and his colleague landed a kick. A hard kick, with his toecap, in the region of the kidneys. Otto Trsnyek groaned feebly and curled up tighter still. Franz closed his eyes. The rushing in his ear had subsided; the pain was almost gone. He suddenly found himself thinking of the worms that, as a boy, he used to pull out of the lush ground after persistent rain, which had always writhed so blindly and pointlessly on his palm. They felt strange, these worms: slippery, taut and cool, and if you pricked them with a sewing needle they curled up very small, and a dark drop welled out of the spot where the needle had gone in.

'Let's try again. How long have you been selling your filthy magazines to the Jews?'

'Always . . .' the tobacconist whispered.

'My dear Mr. Newsagent, one doesn't do such things,' said the mournful man, shaking his head reproachfully. He bent down, seized Otto Trsnyek's head by the hair and slowly raised him up off the floor.

'But it isn't true!' Franz, in the corner, had picked himself up and was standing, on shaky legs. 'The magazines belong to me! I bought them, for myself! All of them! Because I sometimes like to look at things like that.'

'Shut your mouth, Franz!' hissed the tobacconist. 'You've no idea what you're talking about!'

'With all due respect, I know perfectly well. And besides: the truth is the truth and that's all there is to it. And if someone's done something stupid, he must be able to take responsibility for it. Surely you have to admit I'm right there, Mr. Policeman?'

The mournful man dropped Otto Trsnyek's head like a rotten apple. He straightened up and stared at Franz.

'So the best thing is for you to take me with you right now to the police station or the cells or wherever. Because the magazines are my magazines. I bought them and read them, I looked at the pictures, and I hid them in the drawer. And if all that's a crime, I want to answer for it, please.'

'Shut your stupid mouth, you fool!' said the tobacconist, through gritted teeth.

'Why should he?' said the mournful man, affably. 'Let sonny boy have his say. What's his name, anyway?'

'With all due respect, I'm not a sonny boy, and my name is Franz Huchel!'

The mournful man folded his hands behind his back and slunk two or three steps towards Franz. 'Is that so? Well then, say what you have to say, Herr Huchel!'

'Franzl . . .' The tobacconist had raised his head again. His face was contorted with pain, and his gaze wandered among the cigar boxes on the shelves for a few seconds before locating Franz. 'You're my apprentice . . . and you're a fool, as well. Which is why you're going to do exactly what I tell you. Sit back down, and keep your stupid mouth shut!'

Only now did Franz see the thin trail of blood running down his chin, a delicate rivulet, scarcely bigger than a thread. And suddenly he saw the despair in his eyes as well. Like a veil, Franz thought; like a dark, gauzy veil. And at that moment everything became clear. For a fraction of a second a window opened onto the future, and through it white fear blew towards him — him, this small, stupid, powerless boy from the Salzkammergut. With a stifled sob he fell to his knees, put both arms around the tobacconist's neck and pressed his body against him.

'Let me go, Franzl!' Otto Trsnyek whispered hoarsely into Franz's hair. 'Please, let me go!'

When the men had bundled the tobacconist into the back seat, and the car, after repeatedly failing to start, had driven up Währingerstrasse, and turned into Boltzmanngasse, backfiring noisily, Franz remained standing outside the shop. It had started to drizzle lightly, and the smell of wet paving stones rose up beneath the sprinkle of warm spring rain. Somewhere, far away over the rooftops, there was sure to be a rainbow. The tobacconist hadn't shouted or spoken again: he had let them take him away without resistance, hopping to the car supported by the grey men. Franz had run in again to fetch the crutches, but when he brought them back out the men had already driven away. Now the crutches were propped up beside the entrance like two old sticks, lopsided and useless.

The rainwater was running in thin streams down the windowpanes of the Rosshuber butcher's. Behind the glass the butcher's silhouette was sawing at a knuckle of pork. He had stood in his doorway watching with his arms crossed over his bloody apron, lips curled in a smile, watching the tobacconist being carted off. When the car had finally disappeared he had given a brief laugh, shaken his head and gone back inside.

Franz went on standing there, immobile. Maybe that's it, he thought: just stop and stand here like this and never move again. Then time will drift past you, you won't have to swim with it or struggle against it. Pedestrians hurried by without looking at him. Somewhere a child was bawling. Blackbirds were warbling in the flowerbeds around the Votive Church. Two pigeons fluttered up for a moment from a window ledge above Veithammer Installations before huddling back again into their corner by the window. A gust of wind blew a veil of drizzle in Franz's face. Quite pleasant, really, he thought. He closed his eyes and wished never to open them again. Then he heard someone clear their throat behind him and a thin voice say, 'Is anyone here still interested in the customers, or do we have to serve ourselves?'

It was Herr Kollerer, the justice department official. Franz could see a double reflection of himself in Kollerer's thick glasses, with the twin spires of the Votive Church in the background, blurred by a fine mist of rain.

'The shop is open, sir, of course!' said Franz. 'Will it be your usual — the *Wienerwald-Bote*, the *Bauernbündler*, and a Long Heinrich?'

Franz ordered new windowpanes from Staufinger, the master glazier, who delivered them promptly and installed them so that they fitted perfectly. For the first time in many years the tobacconist's was bathed in more than just dim twilight. The brightness from the street penetrated every corner, making the colours on the lids of the cigar boxes glow with new freshness and unaccustomed intensity. However, now the cobwebs and the brownish damp stains on the ceiling were also visible. Franz bought a bucket of white paint, borrowed a ladder, a painting apron and a big horsehair brush from Frau Veithammer, the plumber's wife, and started painting the ceiling. When he had finished doing that he painted the walls and the slats of the chairs, then the shelves, the stationery display case, the box of small goods, the little cupboard for the pipe accessories, the legs of the sales counter, and finally the door and window frames. With the last dollops of paint he retouched the little chips in the varnish on the drawer handles; finally, he dabbed a tiny white dot on the front doorknob, just like that, because it amused him and looked sort of pretty and friendly and artistic. Behind a pile of love-story magazines for the cultivated lady he found Otto Trsnyek's delicately framed, but rather dusty reading glasses. He gave them a spit and polish with his shirtsleeve, wrapped them in newspaper and stored them carefully under the counter. He filled the inkwell, dipped the nib of the fountain pen in a bath of water, sharpened the pencils and smoothed out the dog-ears in the bookkeeping file. He stood on tiptoe by the front door and cleaned and rubbed and polished the little bells until they shone like Christmas tree decorations. On a piece of cardboard, in thick red letters, he painted the words DEAR CUSTOMERS, TRSNYEK'S TOBACCONIST'S IS STILL OPEN — STEP INSIDE, YOU WILL BE SERVED! and stuck the sign on the inside of the door at eye level. He went over to Frau Veithammer's to return the ladder, the brush and the apron, along with a bright yellow flower hastily plucked from the flowerbeds of the Votive Church; he washed the paint off his hands and the dust out of his hair and finally, tired and fragrant with curd soap, he sank into Otto Trsnyek's armchair. He sat there for a few moments listening to the leather creak under his bottom, then took a nice big sheet of squared paper out of the drawer and began to write.

Dear Mama,

This is my first letter to you. Not just to you, in fact; it's my first letter ever. The things I want to write to you won't all fit on a single postcard, you see. Although I don't really know any more what exactly it was I wanted to say. And that's typical at the moment. My mind hasn't been working like it should lately. It feels as if someone's taken my head in their great big hands and given it a violent shake. So — first things first, one after another, nice and slow, from the beginning. It's very pretty here in Vienna. After the long winter the spring is creeping out of every nook and cranny. Everywhere you look something is blooming. The parks look almost like they do on the postcards, and every horse dropping left on the road is bound to produce a daffodil. People are quite mad: they're running about like headless chickens and don't know what they're doing. If you ask me, that's not just because it's spring; it's politics, mainly. These are strange times right now. Or perhaps the times were always strange and I just didn't notice. After all, until recently I was still a child. And I'm not yet a man. And that's the whole problem. Which brings us straight to the next topic: nothing came of it with the girl (the one I wrote to you about!), for now, or for good. Don't ask me why, that's just how it is. Perhaps love isn't meant for me. Perhaps I'm not for love. I don't know. Do you know? Do you know if I'm cut out for love? Do you know what love is? Do you know anything about love? To be honest, it feels pretty strange to ask your own mother such things. Sort of embarrassing. But at this distance it's all right. Anyway, I'm curious to see what you say. By the way, on the subject of distance, you really must write to me about the lake. The postcards are pretty, but pictures are only pictures and can be deceptive. Just like the over-made-up cover-girl faces in the shop. They look at you in a way that makes you think they mean you personally when actually all they're doing is looking into a camera and thinking about a nice juicy beef stew and getting lots of money for it. There, you see: I wasn't exaggerating about my head being badly shaken up. If there'd been a thread running through this letter it would certainly be lost by now, or frayed to pieces, at any rate. So I'd better move on quickly to the next topic. The professor and I are friends now. (That's the truth!) Although we both work almost constantly, we spend as much time together as possible. We sit on the bench, go to the park, and talk about all sorts of things. He smokes. I don't. I ask him about this and that. And he asks me about this or that. Often, neither of us has any answers, but that doesn't matter. Friends are allowed not to have answers sometimes. The age difference doesn't matter to us, incidentally. People can stare and wag their tongues as much as they like — we don't care. Although of course on the other hand the professor really is very old. Sometimes when I look at him I think he's somehow come down to us from ancient times. Like the old plum tree that leans down to the shore behind the cottage, all gnarled and crooked. It doesn't bother me at all that he's a Jew. If Otto Trsnyek hadn't told me, I probably wouldn't even have noticed. In any case, I don't know why everybody is so hard on the Jews. They seem perfectly respectable to me. The truth is, I'm actually a bit worried. About the professor, and generally. Like I said — strange times. Which brings me to another matter, unfortunately quite an unpleasant one. Otto Trsnyek has fallen ill. Not seriously, but still. His liver maybe, or kidneys, or something internal. If you ask me, it's because of the unhealthy food. The food in Vienna is probably even fattier than ours. And you can't do a lot of leaping about with only one leg, in terms of exercise, I mean. Anyway, he's staying at home for a few days for the time being, and we'll have to wait and see. I'll send him your best wishes for a speedy recovery, if that's all right?

    Dear Mama, often I'm sad and I know why. Often, though, I'm sad and I don't know why, and that's almost worse. Sometimes I wish I was back at the lake. Of course I know it's not as simple as that any more. I've already seen and smelled and tasted too much. Life will go on, I just don't know where to yet. And so I'll stop moaning now. Otto Trsnyek's absence means I'm temporarily responsible for managing the shop, so I have to keep looking forward. You can be proud of me, dearest Mama, if you like!
Your Franz

Business didn't completely grind to a halt, but it was bad. The Jewish customers had almost all disappeared. Perhaps, as Franz thought, they had switched to another tobacconist's because of the recent events, or they were sitting in their apartments, keeping quiet, and had temporarily given up reading and smoking. Only old Herr Löwenstein came, as always, to fetch himself a packet or two of Gloriettes. His poor hearing, even worse eyesight, and the general decrepitude that was slowly taking over his body rendered him, as he once said, insusceptible to the events taking over the city; which were not, on the whole, much fun for the people of Moses, he added as he doddered out of the door, chuckling quietly.

But the non-Jewish customers made themselves scarce, too. Presumably because they were waiting to see what would happen with the situation in general and the tobacconist's in particular, which was said to have sold 'erotic magazines' to Jews and was now being run by some funny lad from the sticks. For it was well known that waiting and seeing was always the best, perhaps even the only way to let the various troubles of the times flow past leaving you unscathed.

The few people who did still come had changed. Many now wore brown shirts, some had swastika armbands or at least little swastika pins on their collars, and the majority seemed to go to the barber more frequently than before. They also had a strange light in their eyes. The light was sort of optimistic or hopeful or inspired, but essentially also rather dim-witted; Franz couldn't really make the distinction. In any case, they had this light in their eyes and spoke in loud, clear voices. The muted conversational tone for placing orders or making a purchase that had always suited the shop's gloomy interior so well had been replaced by a brisk, sonorous, rattling inflection. It sounded as if it was only now that the customers really knew what they wanted, or had always been seeking. More and more people greeted each other with 'Heil Hitler!', stretching their arm out as they did so. Franz, to whom this seemed a trifle excessive, got into the habit of replying with a non-committal 'Thank you, same to you!'

He had almost entirely stopped reading the newspapers; in any case, they were nearly all filled with the same, constantly recurring content. If you'd read the *Wienerwald-Bote* you also knew what was in the *Bauernbündler*, had finished the *Reichspost*, didn't need to bother with the *Volksblatt*, and so on. It was as if, every day, the editorial departments gathered for one great big conference in order to maintain at least apparent objectivity by co-ordinating their headlines and incorporating a few differences in the texts of articles that were otherwise wholly identical. They were usually about Adolf Hitler. In no time at all the little man from Upper Austria had occupied the minds of his compatriots, and he certainly wouldn't be leaving again any time soon. They were all completely, idiotically infatuated with the dynamic man with the wiry moustache. Yet Heinzi was definitely the better Hitler, thought Franz; on first impression. He made a much more striking Chancellor of the Reich anyway, one with far more dynamism and far greater charisma. Franz often thought of Monsieur de Caballé with the knife in his trousers. Even more often, though, he thought of Anezka. Sometime he wrote her name on a piece of paper, just like that, in capital letters and Otto Trsnyek's most expensive ink. Or, if he didn't happen to have any paper on hand, in tiny script along the edge of an old newspaper. In a quiet hour after closing time he started writing her name on the palm of his left hand: once, twice, a third time, over and over again. He wrote it on every single finger, on his fingertips, knuckles and the sides of his hands, scrawled it in tiny letters on the folds of the joints, and smaller still under the edges of his nails. When there was no space left on his hand at all he rolled up his sleeve and carried on writing on his arm: Anezka on his wrist, Anezka between the veins and the little hairs on his forearm, Anezka on his elbow, on his upper arm, and in big, wildly looping letters around his shoulder.

One radiant Monday morning in April Heribert Pfründner, the very overweight and so also rather broken-winded postman who had delivered the mail in the Alsergrund/Rossau district for the past thirty-four years, entered the tobacconist's, waited (as he always did) for the little bells to stop ringing, mumbled a slightly grumpy 'Heilitler!' and, along with a couple of leaflets, the local monthly newsletter and an invitation to the official opening of the clubhouse of the First Ottakring Gymnastics Association, tossed an eggshell-yellow envelope onto the sales counter, touched two fingers to his sweating temple in farewell, and panted out again. Franz locked the shop door, retreated to his little room, sat on the edge of his bed and contemplated the envelope, which bore a stamp in the top right corner in

honour of the proud Austrian military leader Radetzky and, to
the left of it, his mother's delicate signature. Fingers trembling
with impatience, he opened it and began to read.

My dear Franzl,

*Thank you so much for your letter. You wrote so beautifully, and
I was really pleased. The weather is warm here. The Schafberg
has a friendly look and the lake is silvery or blue or green, according to its mood. They've planted big swastika flags on the bank.
They reflect in the water and look very correct. In fact everyone
is very correct all of a sudden, running around with important
faces. Just imagine, Hitler hangs on the wall even in the restaurant and the school now. Right next to Jesus. Although we have
no idea what they think of each other. Preininger's lovely car has
been confiscated, unfortunately. That's what they call it these days
when things disappear and reappear again somewhere else. The
car didn't go very far, though. The mayor drives around in it
now. Since the mayor became a Nazi, he's finding a lot of things
easier to do. Everyone wants to be a Nazi all of a sudden. Even
the forest ranger is running around in the forest with a bright
red armband and wondering why he's not shooting anything any
more. Talking of which: do you remember Hannes, our pleasure steamer? They've given it a new coat of paint and rechris-
tened it. Now it glistens like a freshly boiled sweet and is called
'Homecoming'. On its first outing with its new name, though,
the diesel engine exploded and they had to use the old rowing*

boats to bring people back to the shore. Oh, Franzl, my darling boy, what will become of us all? Preininger is dead, and you're so far away. Sometimes I lie in bed and cry into the pillows because there's nobody left for me to look after any more. And nobody to look after me. But nice things happen, too. Guess what: I've found a job! The Goldener Leopold has started letting out a few rooms to guests, and I clean there three times a week. It's not that well-paid, but I sometimes get a tip. Once the innkeeper lay in wait for me and threw me onto one of the guest beds. I told him I was friendly with SS Obersturmbannführer Graleitner from Linz and that he certainly wouldn't be happy about a thing like this. That gave the innkeeper a shock, and he stammered something about a silly misunderstanding. Since then he's left me alone. If he only knew that SS Obersturmbannführer Graleitner was an invention!

I'm very sorry Otto Trsnyek has fallen ill. I hope he gets better soon. Please send him my very best wishes for his recovery. He's a sensitive soul, you know, beneath that grumpy tobacconist exterior. I believe so, anyway. It can't be an easy thing to lose a leg in the trenches. Especially when you ask yourself who it was actually for. It's no wonder if your soul ends up a bit unsteady, too, is it?

To be honest, I don't exactly know what to think of your acquaintance with Herr Professor Freud. I'm not altogether happy about it. I used to be able to forbid you to associate with other boys if I didn't like the look of one of them. Those days are gone. You're old enough now and you must know what you're doing. But please bear this in mind: even if Jews are perfectly respectable, what good does it do them if there's no respectability any more in the world around them?

My dear Franzl, I'm sorry, of course, that nothing came of it with the girl, either for now or for good. Especially as everyone knows how well Bohemians cook. On the other hand: who knows what it was good for! Sometimes you have to let one thing go for another to come. You asked me if I knew anything about love. The truth is: I know nothing about it. Although I have known it. No one knows anything about love, and yet the vast majority of people have known it. Love comes and goes, and you don't understand it beforehand, and you don't understand it afterwards, and you understand it least of all when it's there. And so let me tell you this: no one is cut out for love, and nonetheless, or for precisely that reason, it gets to almost all of us at some point!

It breaks my heart when I hear that you're sometimes sad. What can I tell you? There are as many kinds of sadness as there are hours in our lives. And probably a few more as well. It doesn't make any difference whether you know where this or that sadness comes from. It's part of our lives. If you ask me, even animals are sad. And maybe trees as well. Only stones aren't. They just lie around doing nothing. But who wants that?

My darling Franzl, are you eating enough? You were always so thin! Whenever you jumped in the lake we would completely lose sight of you. Thin and smooth and white, like a young char in spring. I know I shouldn't tell you this, but sometimes I open the

box with your things. Then I pull out one of your old jerseys, hold it up to my face and smell it. I think people get more and more strange as the years go by. I have grey hairs already, but at least my bottom is still reasonably firm. The innkeeper is too stupid and unsavoury for my taste, but in the last few days one of the new tourist guides has been giving me the eye. He's a good-looking chap with a moustache and large hands. We shall see what comes of it. I have to stop now and go over to the inn. A couple of uniforms from Munich have taken up residence; they make a lot of noise and even more dirty laundry. I would so love to send you a tray of potato strudel, but you just don't know with the post these days. My dear, dear boy, you are always in my heart!
Your Mother

Franz ran the tips of his fingers across the lightly ribbed stationery. A peculiar feeling welled up inside him like a fat bubble, percolated along his spine and slipped up the back of his neck into his head, where it floated about softly and pleasantly for a while. *Your Mother*, she had written; not *Your Mama*, like on the postcards, or as she had always done before whenever she left a scribbled note on the kitchen table. Children have mamas; men have mothers. He folded the letter and pressed it to his nose. It smelled of mouldy jetty planks and dry summer reeds, of charred scraps of beef, melted clarified butter and his mother's flour-dusted kitchen apron.

That night Franz dreamed of his late father, a woodsman from Bad Goisern whom he had never known as he was killed by a rotten English oak only a few days before Franz was born. They said he spoke little more in life than in death. In the dream they were walking along a path between quiet fields. Franz was still small and had dust in his hair. The sun burned high above them, and his father merged with his own shadow. They arrived at the big office and entered the shining marble lobby. In the middle sat a fat man furiously stamping his desk pad. A queue of people soon formed in front of him; everyone wanted a stamp, but the fat man wouldn't listen to their begging and pleading. Again and again he brought his stamp whizzing down onto his desk pad. The blows echoed through the room like cannon fire, while the loud blasts of a golden horn announced splendid times to come. Franz's father took him by the hand and tried to push into the queue. He was afraid; his hand was dry and rough like a piece of wood. 'Forgive me,' he kept saying, more to himself than to the people, 'forgive me, forgive me, forgive me.' 'Exactly!' said the fat postal worker triumphantly, and brought his stamp down on Franz's father's forehead. It said FUTURE, and thin trickles of blood ran down between the letters. Franz woke dripping with sweat, and with a peculiar fluttering behind his heart. Still dazed and spiralling out of sleep, he wrote down his dream on a piece of paper:

A walk with Father, the sun is burning, and we go into the big official building where a fat man is stamping away, Father pushes in and excuses himself, the golden horn blares, the fat man stamps the word FUTURE on Father's forehead and cuts him.

He had the piece of paper in front of him on the sales counter all afternoon, and tried not to keep staring at it. This fat man was sort of pathetic, he thought to himself, despite being quite an imposing figure. Pathetic, and a little lonely, too, in his supposed magnificence; and, to cap it all, trapped in the dream of a tobacconist's apprentice he doesn't know from Adam. We ought to be able to see inside people's heads, he thought, but only when they're asleep. During the day you really didn't want to know what was going on in there, and besides, there wasn't a great deal to be expected from the contents of the average head. At night, though, in the quiet hours of darkness, things would look rather different. Caution would no longer stand in the way, and every fear, desire and crazy idea would be free to wander through your brain. Franz would have liked to talk to someone about his dreams, preferably Anezka, or if necessary the professor or Otto Trsnyek, or at the very least one of the customers. But it was gone midday and only two people had entered the tobacconist's. One was Frau Veithammer, who bought herself the latest *Illustrierte Wochenpost* and took the opportunity to complain about her recently deceased husband, who she said couldn't even seem to do things properly in the grave: the flowers above him started withering before they'd even really started to blossom. The other was a little girl, who asked for an HB pencil and counted the coins into Franz's hand one by one with her tiny fingers. Of course, he couldn't expect anything enlightening or otherwise useful from either of them as far as the content of dreams was concerned. But perhaps, thought Franz, the point was not to exchange views on dreams and their possible meaning or probable lack of it. Perhaps the point was to communicate the dreams, entirely without expectation — just to project them, like in a cinema, from the inside of your head onto the empty screen of the outside world, and in doing so to awaken something in observers who either happened to pass by or who approached intentionally; perhaps with a bit of luck, it would even be something of relevance, significance or permanence. He exhaled heavily and sank into the armchair. Blundering about in such dark and unfamiliar trains of thought exhausted him. Through the shop window his eyes fell on the row of houses opposite. One of the windows was almost completely obscured by green plants, and behind it in the gloom a man's white vest was moving back and forth. Franz sighed. He couldn't help thinking of the forest, the soothing murmur of the trees and the tweeting of birds, which never seemed to disturb the quiet despite being noisily omnipresent. A blob of greenish bird shit was stuck to the windowpane at eye level. City birds don't tweet, they screech, he thought morosely. They also shit on your hat and on the shop window and lie down to die in some corner of the attic leaving just their dusty skeleton, a few feathers and a bit of a stench. He sighed again, even deeper than before, and as he was sighing an idea came to him. He fetched some sticky tape from the drawer, took the piece of paper with his dream on it, wrote the date in the top right-hand corner, went out with it onto the street and stuck it on the window right over the blob of shit. He stepped back and regarded the little dream poster. Then he closed his eyes and took a deep breath of the Viennese spring air. For a tiny moment the word FUTURE flashed up behind his eyelids, rosy and bright, like a neon sign at the Prater. Then a delivery van from the United Viennese Ice Factories clattered past on the street behind him, laden with blocks of ice, and he went back inside the shop.

The first people to pay any attention to the curiosity stuck on the shop window of Trsnyek's tobacconist's were three elderly ladies, their wrinkled faces like something carved from a tree root, who craned their necks to get their noses as close to the paper as possible. Franz, sitting motionless in the shadow of the sales counter, watched their eyes narrow until they disappeared almost completely in their wrinkled nests as the withered lips moved in soundless unison to deciphering the words. None of the three seemed to understand a thing. They stood there for a while, toothless mouths agape, then tottered off.

Next to stop in front of the window were two girls in pale

coats. After reading the note they shaded their eyes with their hands like little roofs, leaned their heads against the glass and peered into the shop. When they saw Franz they ran off, giggling. He was still watching the two patches of their breath evaporate from the glass when the next passer-by approached: a workman with an oil-stained face and a crooked roll-up in the corner of his mouth. He scanned the words, frowning, considered for a moment, then entered the tobacconist's and planted himself in front of the sales counter. What was all this about, he wanted to know, this business with the weird scribblings on that piece of paper out there.

Nothing at all, said Franz; at least, nothing in particular.

The workman said he couldn't really believe that, because you didn't go sticking some completely meaningless bilge on the shop window for no reason, just because you were bored or fed up or both.

That may be, said Franz, but something that was significant for one person might be uninteresting or indeed useless to another.

The workman stared at his toecaps and shifted the roll-up thoughtfully to the other corner of his mouth. Did the young tobacconist think he was a fool?, he asked quietly. Someone who couldn't make up his own mind about what was useless or significant to him?

Of course he hadn't meant anything of the sort, Franz answered truthfully. The fools sat elsewhere nowadays.

Where was that, the workman wanted to know.

Everywhere, really, said Franz, just not here in the shop.

The workman nodded. The young tobacconist might well be right about that, he said. Nonetheless, he still wanted to know what this note was all about, goddamn it.

A dream, said Franz. A dream, that was all.

If that was all, said the workman, disappointed, then it *was* useless, at least as far as he was concerned.

That, Franz replied, was precisely what he'd said. However, its possible uselessness had yet to be proved. Because perhaps, he continued, perhaps one day a strange dream note stuck to a shop window, like this one, might have some effect on an observer who happened to pass by, or might move them in some way — you never knew.

Yes, said the workman with a tired sigh, you never did know. For now, though, could he have a packet of Orient tobacco, two boxes of matches and the *Sport-Tagblatt*?

But of course he could, said Franz; that was what a tobacconist's like this was here for, after all.

From then on Franz stuck a new note beside the front door every day. Every morning, before it was time to open the shop, he would step out into the street in his pyjamas, hair tousled with sleep, and stick a freshly dreamed dream on the shop window, still cool from the night. This did not go unremarked. People's curiosity and forgetfulness were still stronger than their fear, and the tobacconist's that, until recently, had sold 'erotic magazines' to Jews and Communists was now just the tobacconist's with the funny little stories on the window. Anyone walking past who happened to spot the note would also stop to read it. Most of them stared at it briefly, expressionless, then walked on. Some said nothing but indicated their disapproval by making a disgusted face. Others shook their heads and shouted a few insults at the shop door. Every now and then, though, Franz would see someone grow a little thoughtful as they read, and saw them quietly take this thoughtfulness away with them.

People read, for example:

April 9, 1938
A song is being sung, it's about love, but the melody is wobbling about all over the place, someone laughs and immediately afterwards jumps off the Votive Church, but the ground is soft, and the flowers are blooming in every colour, no one has seen the dead man, and a crane flies overhead, pulling a cross through the sky.

Or:

April 12, 1938
I'm standing with Mother beside the lake, a steamer is coming towards us, I'm frightened but Mother takes me by the hand — 'IT'S ALL RIGHT, YOU'RE MY CHILD' — but

the steamer keeps coming, the lake sways, Mother has gone, and the steamer crashes into my heart.

Or:

April 15, 1938
A girl is walking through the Prater, she gets on the Ferris wheel, swastikas are flashing everywhere, the girl rises higher and higher, suddenly the roots snap and the Ferris wheel rolls over the city and crushes everything, the girl shrieks with delight, and her dress is flimsy and white like a scrap of cloud.

Frau Dr. Dr. Heinzl, who had switched back to walking on the tobacconist's side of the road, found the paper with the dress 'like a scrap of cloud' particularly noteworthy. She stood in front of the window for a long time, frowning, and read the paragraph several times over. Perhaps she felt reminded of something somehow — impossible to say what. But it can't have been too unpleasant, because when she finally walked off in the direction of Schwarzspanierstrasse with her head slightly bowed, she laughed down at the pavement: a small, high laugh, like dropped jewellery.

One week after Otto Trsnyek was taken away, Franz made his first attempt to contact the tobacconist, or at the very least to discover his whereabouts. The officers at the Alsergrund police

station were friendly, but they had, firstly, no time, and, secondly, other problems. At the City Centre police station the
desk duty officer was far less friendly, but at least he was able
to point Franz in the direction of the office of the recently
established State Secret Police, which was responsible for cases
like these. So Franz set off for Morzinplatz, where the Gestapo
had taken up residence in the former Hotel Metropol, an osten-
tatious building with thick marble pillars outside the entrance.
Three tall swastika standards now clattered before it in the soft
spring air. Behind the windows of the upper floors there was a
bustle of activity: men in uniform or women in grey suits with
bundles of documents in their arms hurried back and forth or
stopped briefly, exchanged a few words, nodded, smiled and
saluted. Every now and then someone would set down his cap
on the window ledge, smoke out into the springtime and let
his gaze drift towards the Kahlenberg. Only on the lowest floor
were the windows dark and blind, hidden behind bars and heavy
metal shutters.

Franz stepped into the entrance hall, where he was immediately approached by a doorman in a blue uniform. 'Might I
perhaps be of some assistance to the young gentleman?'

'I hope so,' said Franz, and listened for a moment to the
way his voice echoed in the vastness of the room. 'My name
is Franz Huchel and I'm looking for a tobacconist called Otto
Trsnyek, who is innocent, but has nonetheless been taken away
or arrested or abducted.'

'First of all, no one in this building is innocent,' said the doorman, twisting his mouth into a forced smile. 'At least, no one who isn't wearing a uniform. Has the young gentleman already made a written application?'

Franz shook his head. 'I didn't actually want to hand in anything at all, I just wanted to fetch the tobacconist Otto Trsnyek and take him back to where he belongs: to his shop!'

'No information without an application,' said the doorman.

Franz looked up at the ceiling, from which hung a huge chandelier decorated with countless little fragments of glass. For a moment it seemed as if the chandelier had started to move and was slowly rotating on its own axis. He lowered his eyes. 'Then I'll come back again,' he said.

'Meaning what?' asked the doorman.

'Then I'll come back again. Tomorrow. The day after tomorrow. The day after that. And so on. Every day at the same time — midday. For as long as it takes until someone tells me where Otto Trsnyek is, how he is, and when I can take him home again.'

And that was what he did. Every day, at twelve o'clock on the dot, he locked the shop, took a little detour along Berggasse (where he secretly hoped to spot the professor's stooping silhouette behind one of the curtains on the first floor), then walked along the Franz-Josef Embankment and over to the former Hotel Metropol, marched up to the doorman through the high-ceilinged entrance hall, and said, 'Good day, I would

like some information as to the whereabouts of the tobacconist Otto Trsnyek!'

For the first few days the doorman continued to make an
effort. Summoning all his official capacities for patience, he
attempted to answer, talking about all manner of authorized
submissions, administrative applications, pre-printed forms
and regular channels. To all of this the impertinent boy always
nodded affably but seemed otherwise quite unmoved, and after
standing there, stubborn as a mule, for about a quarter of an
hour he would politely take his leave, only to reappear punctually at a quarter past twelve the following day asking after this
tobacconist. The doorman's professional equanimity, labori-
ously cultivated over many years of service, began to crumble,
until at last it collapsed altogether. One shimmering Monday
midday, when Franz stood before him once more and said,
'Good day, I would like some information as to the whereabouts
of the tobacconist Otto Trsnyek!', the doorman replied with a
barely perceptible shrug. Then he reached for the receiver of
the black telephone on the wall behind him, dialled a two-fig-
ure number and murmured a few unintelligible words into
the receiver. About ten silent seconds later, a hidden door flew
open in the wall beside the telephone, and a man in a beige
linen suit came out. He seemed to be smiling as he walked
towards Franz, but on closer inspection it was just a shadow
under his little pale blond, almost white moustache. A shadow
smile, Franz was thinking; and then the man was beside him.

He yanked his head back by the hair, twisted his arm onto his back in a single swift movement, and dragged him through the entrance hall out into the open.

Franz felt the pavement beneath his heels and the man's hand gripping his lower arm like a log clamp. He saw the slightly overcast sky above him and the three swastika standards. Then there was a jolt, his arm was suddenly free, and a moment later he hit the ground face first. He fell into a black hole and was aware of a peculiar sound. Like a damp twig in the fire, he thought, just before he went under. When he resurfaced into the light a few seconds later, he was staring straight at the blond man's shoes. They were shiny, polished loafers, made of soft leather and expensively sewn. Not a crack, not a mark, not a speck of dust, only fine, smooth, immaculate leather. Franz lifted his head and looked the man in the face. Seen from this perspective, with the bright midday sky behind him, the little moustache looked as if it were made of quivering raffia. The doorman's blue-capped head loomed up alongside it.

'Perhaps it would be better if the young gentleman didn't come here any more. Otherwise he might find . . .' He left a long pause, in which he made a performance of clearing his throat and blinking invisible irritants from his eyes. 'Otherwise he might find himself staying as a guest of the Hotel Metropol for rather longer than he would like. Has the young gentleman understood?' Franz nodded. The doorman took a snow-white handkerchief from his breast pocket, carefully unfolded it and held it up against the light like an awning, touching the finely embroidered hem and the neatly ironed folds with the tip of his ring finger. Then he bent down, pressed it into Franz's hand and said, 'Wipe the blood off your face, sonny boy. And go home.'

Only when they had both disappeared back inside the building did Franz press the handkerchief to his mouth. The material was immediately soaked in bright blood. His tongue was swollen and felt hot and alien in his mouth. One of his front teeth was wobbly. Gingerly, Franz took it between the tips of his fingers and pulled. It yielded with a little tug. It was a beautiful, straight tooth. Only the root was broken, jagged and bloody. He would put it in the drawer of his bedside table, thought Franz, right beside the postcards and the letter from his mother and the little body of the moth that fell out of the night.

Three weeks later, on the morning of the seventeenth of May 1938, summer declared itself. A pleasantly balmy breeze swept the chill of the night from the streets and across the Danube, far out onto the Schwechat plain. All across the city windows were opened, and blankets and pillows were shaken out, down feathers hovering in the air like white blossom. Early in the morning shift workers and housewives were queuing up out-side the bakeries, and the streets smelled of fresh bread rolls and coffee. The first trams squeaked lethargically out of their sheds, and here and there droppings from the horses on the milk carts steamed on the cobbles. The stallholders at the Naschmarkt had set out their wares hours ago, and at the aged stall of the even more aged Herr Podgacék the first pensioners were arguing over the biggest heads of cauliflower and the mealiest potatoes. On the Prater's main boulevard the weight-lifters from the tram workers' sports association were meeting for their final open-air training session before the big compe-tition against SV Germania. Listlessly extending and stretching their limbs, they gazed up, yawning, over the chestnut trees to where the Ferris wheel cabins shone in the morning sun. In the basement of the Gestapo office, in the former laundry room of the Hotel Metropol, fifteen Jewish businessmen were made to strip and wait with their hands above their heads to be fetched for individual interrogation. Their clothes lay in a heap in the middle of the room, topped by a checked, crum-pled cap like that of an American silent film comedian. On Platform II at Vienna West Station, four hundred and fifty-two political prisoners sat crammed together in the rear carriages of a specially chartered train, awaiting departure for Dachau. On the opposite platform, an old woman and a small boy sat beside each other on a bench, taking alternate bites from a large slice of bread and butter. High above them, under the station roof, a few swallows tumbled from a shadowy corner, hurtled off into the open and disappeared in the direction of Hütteldorf. When the whistle shrilled to signal its departure and the train began to move, the boy hopped off the bench and ran along the platform, waving and laughing. At that moment, something curious happened: all the prisoners at the windows waved back. The boy ran to the end of the platform, then stood still and shielded his eyes with his hand. Even at a distance, as the train gradually dissolved in the morning sunlight, it looked like a huge caterpillar with countless waving legs, crawling away.

At around this time the postman Heribert Pfründner was panting up Berggasse with his postbag, which weighed a ton. He was sweating heavily, his stomach ached, and he still had the taste of his wife's breakfast coffee in his mouth: stale, insipid, and slightly bitter. Much like a postman's life in general, thought Heribert Pfründner morosely; before nine in the morning, anyway. Ever since the Nazis had ensconced themselves in the central post office, the people of Vienna had been receiving their letters at the crack of dawn, which meant that Heribert Pfründner, like his colleagues, had to crawl out of bed an hour earlier, and the coffee seemed to slop about in his stomach even more stalely, insipidly and bitterly than it already had over his past thirty-three years of service. One could be sitting beside a lake or a pool, he thought, or at least some pond in the Wienerwald not too infested with mosquitoes, dipping one's swollen feet in the water and thinking of nothing, or lying on the banks of the Danube, anyway, drinking a third glass of beer and watching time sluggishly pass one by.

The two plainclothes policemen were hanging around in front of Berggasse 19, as they had done for the past few weeks, shifty characters with shadowed eyes and nicotine-yellow faces. 'Heilhitler!' murmured the postman, his sweaty hands fumbling with the bunch of keys in order to unlock the door and get to the letterboxes. This time, too, they stopped him. They always stopped him. They always wanted to know what was in his postbag. They always made him show them the letters, particularly those addressed to Professor Sigmund Freud; they held the envelopes up to the light, deciphered the sender and tried, feeling with their nicotine-yellow fingers, to determine the contents. They always kept one or more for themselves. Today it was two: a big, heavy envelope addressed in flowing handwriting, written with a fountain pen, to 'The most esteemed Herr Professor Dr. Freud', and a little pale blue letter with slightly battered corners. Probably from England, thought Heribert Pfründner, or Sweden, perhaps; from some country, anyway, that had a king on its stamps with a serious yet somehow kindly expression. He unlocked the door, hastily put the post in the letterboxes, and left with a wordless nod. The suspicious letters had long since vanished into the plainclothes policemen's baggy pockets. And who knew, thought Heribert Pfründner, they might even be right: after all, this Freud was a professor, firstly, and secondly a Jew, and as everyone knew, you never could tell with either. What was certain, though, was that he was the post office's best customer in this sector. Accordingly, the bag lost much of its weight after the delivery to Berggasse 19; today, too, making the remainder of his round far more agreeable and easy to cope with. When the postman Heribert Pfründner finally turned into Währingerstrasse and saw before him the skinny figure of the young tobacconist Franz Huchel stepping outside into the clear early morning light, he could already feel in his calves that refreshingly cool, buoyant sensation that heralded the imminent end of his shift.

Franz had been tossing and turning all night in a tumult of dreams, a rushing confusion of words, sounds and images. Waking was deliverance, and although the memory began to dissolve with his first sleepy blinks like shreds of fog at daybreak, he had struggled to get at least a few words of this chaos down on paper. Shortly afterwards, still a little bleary-eyed, he stepped out of the tobacconist's and stuck the note on the window. A sudden, sharp pain briefly shot through his mouth. The swelling in his tongue and jaw had gone down just a few days after his last visit to the Gestapo, and he had grown more or less accustomed to the new gap in his mouth. Secretly, he even liked his missing tooth, and as he played with it with the tip of his tongue, feeling the smooth sides of the adjacent teeth and the soft, warm floor of the gum as it slowly healed, he thought of Anezka: her teeth, her gap, her rosy tongue.

'Heilitler! May I?' The postman, who had come up behind

him on soft-soled shoes, leaned in close to the window, expertly feigning interest, and read:

May 17, 1938
A tram is ringing through the wood, the rabbits' eyes are dark drops, cabins are hanging in the trees, and white fear crouches above the clouds, something is gnawing at my roots, perhaps we should have extinguished the embers?

'Aha,' said the postman, who had frozen slightly. He tried to recover himself. 'Interesting. Especially the bit with the rabbit!'

'Yes,' said Franz. 'Do you have any post for me?'

'Oh, right — of course,' nodded the postman, and took out of his agreeably limp bag the last parcel of his daily round: a longish box, wrapped in brown packing paper and neatly taped. 'Here you are: an official package today, if you please!'

Franz took the parcel and thanked him. With a brief grunt, probably intended to signify benevolent friendliness, the postman touched his cap and set off, light of foot, on the final hundred metres of his path, chasing happy thoughts of the first beer of the afternoon.

Franz took the parcel inside, put it on the sales counter and looked at it in the light of the little lamp. The consignment was addressed to him personally. *To Herr Franz Huchel, Management of Trsnyek's Tobacconist's, Vienna 9, Währingerstrasse*. An official blue stamp announced the sender: *The Inspector of the Security*

Police, Vienna 1, Morzinplatz 4. For a moment Franz was aware that the word 'Management' made his chest to expand with a pleasantly warm feeling of pride; then he ripped at the parcel and opened the box. The covering letter lay right on top: typed, it too bore the official blue stamp, and an indecipherable signature.

The Head of the Security Police Vienna I, the ....**16th May 1938**.....
............**L VII — 75 / 39g**.............

Please quote date and reference above when replying.

To:
Herr Franz Huchel
Manager of
Trsnyek's Tobacconist's
Währingerstrasse
Vienna 9

Re: Return of personal items/valuables

Enclosure: 1

We would like to take this opportunity to inform you herewith of the decease of your acquaintance, the tobacconist Herr Otto Trsnyek. Herr T. succumbed to his unspecifiable heart condition on the night of 13th/14th May on the premises of Gestapo Headquarters, Vienna 1, Morzinplatz 4. Interment by the City of Vienna took place on 15th May 1938 at the Vienna Central Cemetery, Group 40, Row IV/2.

In April of this year a criminal file was opened on Herr T.
He was arrested and charged

on suspicion of subversive activities,
with crimes against public order and breach of the peace,
with crimes according to the Treachery Act,
with the illegal possession of official party stamps.

A decision regarding the seizure and confiscation of property and financial assets (if extant) will be made in the coming weeks. Until then, all rights and claims of third parties
on these property and financial assets are unlawful. For this
period Herr Franz Huchel, b. 7th August 1920 in Nussdorf
am Attersee, is authorized by interim order to make the
necessary provisions for the maintenance of the business
and to take over the temporary management of Trsnyek's
Tobacconist's. In discharge of our obligation, we are return-
ing to you Herr Trsnyek's personal effects, namely:

1 bunch of keys
1 wallet (empty)
1 photograph (person unknown)
1 woollen cardigan
1 shoe
1 pair trousers (damaged)

CC   Signed ....
B/MA/G   Admin. Dir. Dr. Kernsteiner

Franz placed the letter on top of a pile of magazines for the
modern woman and spread out the items on the sales counter:
the shoe in the middle, the bundled cardigan to the left of it,
the bunch of keys at the top on the edge of the blotting pad,

the wallet beside the inkwell, and the photo right in the cone of light from the desk lamp. The picture showed Otto Trsnyek as a young man in uniform, standing and leaning against a brick wall. His left leg was bent and propped against the wall. His cap hung next to his shoulder, on a nail, perhaps, or a shoddily laid brick. He looked tired. He seemed to want to surrender the weight of his whole body to the wall. He was looking past the camera, somewhere off into the distance. The things looked nice laid out on the counter. He should get someone to paint them, thought Franz; or hire the photographer from the pony carousel — he could take a photo of them. A little tobacconist still-life. He took the neatly-folded trousers, shook them out in front of his chest, held them up to the shop window and let the truncated leg dangle against the light. The fabric was thin and threadbare. If the tobacconist had worn the trousers a little longer his knee would soon have been able to see out, as if through a small, daintily barred window. Franz put them back on the sales counter, locked up, and went to his little room. He closed the door behind him and stared into the darkness for a while. Suddenly his legs gave way beneath him, and he sank to the floor beside the bed, where he lay and cried until he had no tears left.

Shortly before closing time he got up and went back into the shop. He folded up Otto Trsnyek's trousers and took them with him to Rosshuber's butcher's. The butcher and his wife were standing behind the counter pressing heavy chunks of meat and fat through a grinder. Frau Rosshuber was stuffing the dark red, yellow, and bluish lumps in on one side, while on the other her husband received the sluggish torrent of rosy worms, moulded them into heaps, wrapped them in grease-proof paper and slapped the fist-sized packages down beside one another on a tin tray. When the door opened and the tobacconist's boy from next door came in they didn't even raise their heads; they just bent even more diligently over the machine. But when Franz pushed open the little swing door next to the refrigerator and approached them behind the counter — just like that, without a greeting, without asking, without saying anything at all — they stopped short, straight-ened up, stepped back, and crossed their bloodstained arms over their bloodstained aprons.

'What d'you want?' asked the butcher, staring at the floor tiles, where blood and melted ice converged in peculiar streaks.

Franz placed the trousers next to the greasy packets on the tray and said, 'These belonged to Otto Trsnyek. Now he's dead.'

Rosshuber turned pale. Like marble, thought Franz, like one of those marble saints that stand around in churches star-ing at people with their cold stone eyes: big, stiff and pale. The butcher opened his small child's mouth. His teeth were narrow and yellow, the gums as rosy as the meat worms still crawling out of the machine behind him. 'And what have we got to do with it?' he asked.

'You defaced his shop,' said Franz. 'You insulted him. You betrayed him. And you killed him!'

The butcher raised his heavy head and stared dumbly at Franz's brow.

'Go on, say something!' said his wife, nervously wiping some morsels of mince off her arms. Rosshuber raised his shoulders, dropped them again, snorted, tweaked his apron, stared into space, snorted again, was silent.

'Perhaps he's got nothing more to say.' Franz stepped right up to the butcher and looked him straight in the eyes. The marble cheeks were suffused with pink spots, and a glittering bubble of spit clung to the corner of his mouth. Franz raised his hands and contemplated the smooth skin on the back. 'My mother always said I had very delicate hands. Delicate, white and soft, like a girl's. I never wanted to hear that, but now I think she was right.' He let them fall again. Then he drew back his right hand and gave the butcher a resounding slap in the face.

Rosshuber didn't move. He didn't move and he didn't make a sound. He just stood there, heavy, silent and immobile, and stared straight through Franz. The little bubble in the corner of his mouth had burst. His cheek had reddened slightly, and two slim marks were visible below the cheekbone.

'Eduard!' said his wife, her face contorted with horror, breaking the chilly silence in the room.

But the butcher did nothing. Only long after Franz had

tucked Otto Trsnyek's trousers under his arm and left the shop did he move again. Very slowly he raised both hands and, with a long-drawn-out, muffled groan, lowered his face into his palms.

Dear Mama,

I would have liked to send you another postcard (a few new ones have arrived, particularly impressive ones, with St. Charles' Church, geraniums, the Gloriette and so on). But some words can't take pictures; they need an envelope. I can't say it any better, so I'll just say it like it is. Otto Trsnyek died yesterday. His heart just stopped beating. Perhaps it didn't want to carry on, with this life, with the times, and with everything else. He probably didn't notice a thing. He went to sleep quite peacefully. In Burgenland, where he's from. Please, dear Mama, don't be sad. Or please do be sad. Otto Trsnyek deserves that. But you know that better than I do, anyway. I'm staying here for the time being. Because what else am I to do? Besides, someone has to run the tobacconist's. Things have to keep going. And there really is plenty to do. Everything all around is in some kind of upheaval, it seems to me. I just hope it doesn't all fall apart. What doesn't change is the lake. The mountains and the clouds will reflect in it longer than those few skinny swastika flagpoles, believe me! Dear Mama, I'll end this sad letter here, with a warm hug. Your Franz

The silence and vast expanse, thought Franz, as he sat on a lightning-blackened tree trunk near the Stefaniewarte observation point on top of the Kahlenberg, looking down on Vienna: the silence and vast expanse, the clarity and depths, the mistiness and mysteriousness, the sun, the rain, the city, the lake, the mountain. Although of course this Kahlenberg isn't a mountain, he thought, at least not a mountain you can take seriously, like the Schafberg, for example, or the Hochleckenkogel, or even the Höllengebirge range. In the Salzkammergut the Kahlenberg would be considered a hill, if that. An insignificant elevation, rather, or a rise, or just a great pile of earth with pretty sparse forest cover. But the Viennese think otherwise, he thought. For the Viennese, the Kahlenberg is not only a real mountain, it's also the highest and most beautiful mountain in the whole region — and, on Sundays and holidays in particular, the most overrun by the nature-hungry population.

Now, though, in the early evening of a perfectly ordinary weekday, there wasn't a soul to be seen. No one stumbling about in the undergrowth in search of peace and quiet or chanterelle mushrooms; no one trying to summon his dachshund, his children and his own good humour; and no one spreading out a woollen blanket to enjoy a late-afternoon snack accompanied by the traditional bottles of warm beer. Franz was alone. And even if the Kahlenberg was just God's botched copy of a real mountain, it was still kind of nice up here. You could sit quietly and let your thoughts wander; it smelled of sun and forest, and only the faintest hint of the otherwise ever-present roar of the city made its way up here. After his brief visit

to the butcher's he had returned to the tobacconist's, written
his second ever letter to his mother, then packed the tobacconist's effects nice and neatly — apart from the trousers —
in a large cigarette box, stuck a piece of paper on it labelled
HERR OTTO TRSNYEK'S LAST THINGS, and stowed it under the
sales counter. He had served the customers, taken receipt of a
delivery of schoolbooks (forty pages, twenty pages, plain, lined,
squared, with and without margins), and turned the high-qual-
ity cigars in their boxes to protect them from the damp. Above
all, though, he had read the newspapers again for the first time
in ages; if not all, then at least most of them, and if not from
cover to cover, then at least in greater part. Finally, punctually
at six o'clock, he had started to do the day's bookkeeping. But
even as he was unscrewing the cap of Otto Trsnyek's fountain
pen he felt somehow strange; then, as he was scribbling the first
figures into the accounts, he was overwhelmed by an unfamiliar, painful yearning and his hand started to shake so hard that
three fat drops of ink fell from the pen nib one after another,
making three spiky, blue-black blots right in the middle of the
balance column. Franz wanted to get out, outside, into the open
air, into the forest, up the mountain, even if the mountain was
just a mound of earth on the outskirts of Vienna. He screwed
the fountain pen shut again, not even troubling to dab up the
ink blots with his little sponge, locked the shop and hurried out
towards the Kahlenberg, walking into the spicy wind.

The tree trunk he was sitting on was still warm from the

sun and smelled pleasantly of mould. In one spot red beetles crawled over one another, crept under a piece of rotten bark, re-emerged, disappeared again. Those who knew nothing had no worries, thought Franz, but if it was hard enough painstakingly to acquire knowledge, it was even harder, if not practically impossible, to forget what you had once known. He let one of the beetles crawl onto his forefinger. It immediately started running madly round his fingertip. Carefully he set it down again on the piece of bark and watched it disappear in the seething mass. The beetles' backs looked like little heraldic shields, their legs like tiny, twitching letters continually forming new words, sentences, stories, as they scrabbled over the moist earth of the Kahlenberg. He was reminded of the newspapers, the headlines. Such a commotion, such a lot of shouting in print. And yet they seemed to be saying that everything was just fine: basically, everything was going splendidly, wonderfully, excellently, in fact it was truly fantastic! Of course, history was being made right now — but when was it not? There were big changes taking place — but they were necessary, weren't they? Communists' and unconventional thinkers' subversive assets were being seized — but wasn't that only fair? Jewish people's property was being confiscated, their shops closed and managed by good, upright citizens — but weren't these just long overdue measures to maintain public security and order in our lovely city of Vienna? In our tolerant state of Austria, so beloved of God? Things are moving forward! Things are

happening! Everywhere there's something going on! Opening
of the *Degenerate Art* exhibition in the Künstlerhaus! Shocking!
The Führer in Italy! The Führer in Munich! The Führer in
Salzburg! The Führer everywhere! Incredible! Mussolini gives
a speech! Goebbels speaks in Düsseldorf! Excellent! Jewish
insurgents challenge Britain! The Reich Railways Shooting
Club tournament is taking place in Vienna's Kagran district!
A Communist kills himself! And another! And another! But
didn't they deserve it, dear readers, just a little? Big flower show
today in Favoriten district! Free entry for children and veter-
ans! Where else would you find such a thing! The authorities
are going to purge the Prater of foreign riffraff! Free beer for
everyone today! Big aeronautical show tomorrow! Everybody
come! Come and watch! Bring your family! Have you already
laughed today? Our photograph shows the Führer viewing
the impregnable bunker! The weather in the Ostmark: windy
with scattered cloud! At the theatre tonight: *Behave Yourself,
Lisa!* (comedy)! At the cinema tomorrow: *The Clever Stepmother*
(comedy)! The world is turning! Everything's fine! A child was
born in the cinema yesterday! Three cheers! The Gestapo is
celebrating its anniversary! Soon it'll be Mother's Day! Soon
it'll be Christmas! 'Heaven, Vienna mine, / I'm in the spell of
your charms divine!'

Franz looked out over the city. The sun was low, the roofs
were shining, here and there a stray sunbeam flashed up at
him, and the Danube wound its silvery way between the houses

before disappearing in the wide, dark meadows. The tobacco-nist's shop must be over there somewhere. Next to it the Votive Church. Morzinplatz. The Opera. The Prater with the Giant Ferris Wheel. The Ferris wheel, in whose shadow the show was about to begin. Any moment now the lizard man would close the doors. The girl with the scar would run her cloth once more over the tables damp with beer and schnapps and then switch on the spotlights. Monsieur de Caballé would come on stage. The jokes. Hitler. The dog. The wonderful gramophone. N'Djina, the shy girl from the land of the Indians. Everything as it always was; everything was as before. He closed his eyes. What was one supposed to think, on a day like this, in times like these, alone on top of a mountain that wasn't a mountain at all, with a few red beetles at one's feet and a city gone mad? Anything was conceivable. Anything was possible. Those who sweep the riff-raff off the streets and blast the Jewish rats out of their holes, who plant swastikas on the shore of the lake and give a steamer the name 'Homecoming', who kill tobacco-nists and throw mothers onto unmade beds, who by day point legions of hands at the sky above Heldenplatz by day and by night run braying down the alleyways — such people would lift the Giant Ferris Wheel off its hinges, too, or stamp the little green grotto into the ground.

All at once Franz felt a pain in his left hand, a slight sting-ing in his fingers, on the tips, sides and knuckles. Tiny points of flame that swiftly multiplied and branched off into fine, glowing lines: over his wrist, his forearm, his upper arm, his shoulder. Hundreds of delicate, fountain-pen-nib-like, brightly burning signatures. *Anezka*, thought Franz, *Anezka*. He started running. Desperately he hurled himself down the slope. The ground beneath his feet was soft and damp; the rocks were overgrown with dark moss and the treetops rustled above him. He ran as fast as he could, hearing his own breath like the panting of a stranger. And for a moment he no longer knew whether the twigs that hit him in the face, chest and arms were real, or whether he was trapped in his own dream; whether he was wide awake or dreaming as he flew down the steep slopes of the Kahlenberg.

When Franz entered the grotto an hour later, breathless, his shoes covered with mud, the show was already coming to an end. The lizard stretched his head forward, gave him a fifty percent discount and opened the hidden door. Apparently N'Djina had already finished her dance and left the stage. The men's beer-dulled eyes still glowed with the spark she had lit in them. A pudgy, balding man stood in the spotlight. He was wearing a lemon-yellow suit, waving his arms in the air and addressing the audience in a hoarse falsetto. The girl with the scar stood behind the counter. Her face flickered in the candlelight; the scar on her cheek, sharp and dark, looked as if it had been drawn on. She greeted Franz with a brief nod. At a table in the background sat three men in black uniforms. One of them, a young man with bland features and pasty skin, wore a dagger on his hip attached to a chain of little silver skulls. On stage, the master of ceremonies told a joke. What could one expect of a Jewess's housekeeping these days? he wanted to know. Someone bawled out the answer, everyone laughed and clapped, and the lemon-yellow man looked astonished. Franz circled around the stage and disappeared through the door behind it. At the end of a dark corridor was another door. A strip of light shimmered out from underneath, and the hinges creaked slightly when he opened it. The room was tiny and brightly lit; there was a smell of sweat and makeup. Anezka was sitting at a table against the wall, facing a mirror surrounded by little brightly coloured lights. She was still wearing her costume, and the feather in her hair quivered as Franz came in. 'Ah, sonny boy!' she said with a smile, wiping the warpaint off her cheeks with a little sponge.

'Anezka,' said Franz, and the name felt strangely foreign, as if he had never said it out loud before. 'Where's Heinzi?'

She shrugged. 'Gone. Taken by Gestapo.'

'Why?'

'Because of jokes. And other things.'

Franz stared at her reflection. In one place the mirror was broken and a piece of glass was missing. It looked as if she had a dark dent in her forehead.

'Have you had a parcel already?' he asked quietly.

'What sort parcel?'

He swallowed. 'Don't know. Nothing. It's probably just non-sense . . .' She had wiped off all the colour now, and she started spreading a dab of white cream over her forehead and cheeks with the tip of her finger. The white made her face look a bit like a mask. Franz was reminded of the death mask that hung behind the altar of the chapel in Nussdorf. It depicted some village saint whose name and origins, as well as the reasons for his supposed beatification, had been forgotten over the years. Its expression as it stared out into the body of the church was either friendly or crafty, depending on the angle and the fall of the light, and it frightened the children during Sunday mass. In fact, everyone disliked it, but so far no priest had dared to take it down and put it with the moth-eaten old prayer books in the box in the cellar of the church: after all, you never really knew, and it was better to be safe than sorry, because God moves in mysterious ways.

Anezka had rubbed in the cream. She loosened a couple of hairpins, pulled the wig off her head in one swift movement and hung it on a hook beside the mirror. She brushed the hair back from her forehead and looked at Franz, her face rosy and shining.

'Where did tooth go?' she asked.

'Don't know,' said Franz, probing the smooth gum with the tip of his tongue. Anezka put down the brush, stood up and came very close to him. He could smell her makeup, her skin, her sweat, her breath.

'Have pretty gap in teeth!' she said, and laughed. 'Look like me now!'

'Yes,' said Franz, and gulped. Suddenly he felt overcome by a slight giddiness. Perhaps it was the stuffy air in the grotto. Perhaps he had run too fast. He took a step forward, then two to the right, and stared for a moment at the wall. Strange, he thought, that it was possible to get lost in such a small room. The wall was roughly plastered and covered in stains. In one place there was a hook with a frayed thread hanging from it, moving slightly. Franz could feel his heart, a big, warm throbbing in his breast. He must have outrun it somewhere coming down the Kahlenberg or in the streets on the outskirts of town, and it had only just caught up with him. The thread stopped moving. The giddiness had passed. Franz turned, took two steps back towards Anezka, put a hand on her cheek and began to speak without thinking, the words pouring out of him: 'Anezka, I don't understand it myself, everyone's gone mad, people are throwing themselves off roofs, they've killed Otto Trsnyek, and who knows what's happening to Heinzi right now, the Jews are kneeling on the pavement cleaning the paving stones, it'll be the Hungarians next or the Burgenlanders or the Bohemians or, I don't know, anyone who hasn't got the swastika branded on their brain is in for it, anyone who won't point their arm at the sky might as well book in to the Hotel Metropol right away, a room with a one-way ticket; the dancing's over in Vienna and the Black Death is going round the Prater, haven't you seen, they're sitting out front already, drinking their beer and just waiting to hurl the next tobacconist or Jew or joke-teller onto the bonfire, Anezka, I don't know if you still want me, and I don't know if I still want you, it doesn't matter any more, the SS are sitting out there jingling their spurs, but perhaps we can go away, the two of us, I mean, somewhere where it's quiet, to Bohemia if you like, behind the dark hill, or to the Salzkammergut, I'm sure Mama wouldn't mind, I could open a tobacconist's, and we could get married, just like that, because it's all the same to God, anyway, and then you'd be a . . .'

At that moment the door opened and the pasty young man entered the room. He had his cap clamped under his arm and was looking around with interest. The little skulls clicked on the chain of his dagger. Franz felt the muscles tense up at the back of his neck. Right, he thought: any minute now the door will open again and more black uniforms will come crashing in. Or creep in silently like big black birds. He would have liked just to run out of the dressing room and out of the grotto, all the way back, up the Kahlenberg, straight down the other side and on and on, along the Danube, back to its source and beyond. But that was no longer possible. Here he stood. Here stood Anezka. And that was all. He breathed out, deeply, and in, deeply, then stepped forward, crossed his arms over his chest and said, 'My dear sir, I would like to inform you, in all politeness, that it honestly doesn't matter to me whether you're wearing a black uniform or a blue or a yellow one, or whether you have skulls or pebbles or sneaky thoughts dangling round your belly. This Bohemian girl here, on the other hand, matters to me very much. She's an artist, you see, and she hasn't done anything to anyone. Other than kissing, or rather, awakening me, which means she is under my personal protection. So I would like to implore you most sincerely, dear sir, to please just leave us alone. And if there's absolutely no way round it and you simply have to bring back something for your Sturmführer or Bannführer or Sturmbannführer or some other Führer, then in God's name, take me!'

The young man blinked. His eyelashes were long and softly curved, his forehead high, smooth and white. He glanced at Anezka. She sighed, appeared to consider for a moment, blew a stray lock of hair off her forehead and sighed again. Then she walked over to him, put both arms around him, snuggled up and laid her cheek on his shoulder where two thick white cords dangled from the epaulettes.

'Oh, so that's how it is,' said Franz, after a while.

Anezka blinked languidly. 'Yes, that's how it is,' she replied.

Franz looked up at the ceiling. A thought briefly crept into his mind, as filthy and squalid as the matted bits of fluff peeping out between the cracks in the boards, but he chased it away again. Instead, he would have liked to tear a hole in the wall with his bare hands; he would simply have walked out through it and on just a few alleys further over, as far as the Giant Ferris Wheel. He would have liked to get into one of the cabins and let himself be carried round and round in a circle until the pain had gone. Anezka's rosy forefinger played with the cords at her cheek. The young man had put his hand on the back of her neck and began to stroke her hairline.

'Perhaps we should . . .' said Franz, and faltered.

'What?' asked Anezka. She placed her hand over the hand on her neck.

Franz shrugged. 'I don't know,' he said. 'I really don't know.' Then he turned and left.

As he pushed past the tables, heading for the exit, the lemon-yellow master of ceremonies was executing an elegant bow and waving his hat above his bald and sweaty head. Long after Franz had left the grotto and was slowly heading up the narrow, fenced alleyway towards the Giant Ferris Wheel, he could still hear the muffled applause behind him. It made him think of the bats he had watched so often as a boy: all day they hung, almost motionless, from the roofs of the limestone caves in Unterach, only to detach themselves just after sunset as if at a silent signal and swoop out into the night in a gigantic swarm.

Since the Nazis had definitively been calling the shots all over Vienna — and so in the central post office too, of course — not everything had changed for the worse, the postman Heribert Pfründner thought as he trudged the last few metres up Berggasse. Admittedly, some things might even have changed for the better; you had to give them that much, to be fair. For

example, they'd changed the word for 'postage stamps', and the
new stamps were now much prettier, more colourful and somehow more impressive, with the eagles and the crowds and the
Danzig coat of arms and all the other stuff. Some stamps had a
picture of the Führer now, too. Basically, despite all that fervent
German nationalism, the Führer was still an Austrian, thought
Heribert Pfründner, a true Upper Austrian from the nice though
really quite unremarkable town of Braunau am Inn, so he'd
know what was good for a country like this, with all its residents
and its post office customers. Because if the Führer didn't know
what he was doing he wouldn't be a Führer; he'd be mayor, or
head of the local council, or treasurer of the local council of
Braunau am Inn, at best. Some things did seem rather dubious,
though, he thought, listening to the tinny sounds made by the
envelopes and postcards as he dropped them into the letterboxes
in the house on the corner of Berggasse and Währingerstrasse.
For example, these stories you heard more and more often lately
about the Jews. After all, wasn't it a bit disgraceful, actually, to
throw the Jews out of their apartments, businesses and official
positions, and especially out of all the post offices, and then
make them shuffle up and down the pavement on their knees
as well? Or that bad business with the letters that people were
whispering about at work. Word had it that there was a vast
basement underneath the central post office, rooms with
blinding lights where hundreds of men and women worked in
shifts, opening letters and, depending on the contents, either

releasing them for delivery or passing them on to the postal authorities for closer examination. And it was true that almost every other letter you delivered nowadays had been slit open, which of course was nothing but a complete and utter disgrace for every halfway respectable postman and thus especially for him, Heribert Pfründner, who was, as everybody knew, the most respectable postman in the Alsergrund/Rossau district. But then, he thought, what did all this have to do with him? It had been a long time since he received any post himself, and somehow or other he would gasp his way through the few remaining years until retirement. Besides, he wasn't a Jew; he was originally from Upper Styria, and so had a spotless family tree that could be traced right back to the Stone Age.

Lost in these thoughts, and other, quite different ones, Heribert Pfründner had finally arrived outside the little tobacconist's on Währingerstrasse. From his postbag, which now hung nice and loose on his shoulder, he dug out a copy of the Alsergrund local newsletter and a few brightly coloured brochures, shot a quick glance at that day's dream note on the windowpane, pushed open the door and entered the shop with what was for him a fairly cheerfully mumbled 'Heilitler!'

Behind the counter Franz looked up from his bookkeeping, which he had been struggling with half the night and all of the morning, and gave the postman a nod. 'Mr. Postman,' he said wearily, 'as far as Hitler's concerned, you can stick him you know where. That aside, I wish you a good morning!'

Heribert Pfründner acted as if he hadn't heard. He cleared his throat awkwardly, the leather shoulder strap on his bag creaking a little, looked around at the newspaper shelves, yawned, tugged at the knot of his tie, and cleared his throat again.

'I'm sure you'll have heard,' he said at last, leaning in a little closer to the sales counter. 'Since you're a close acquaintance, as it were, of the Herr Professor.'

'Of which professor?'

'Well — the idiot doctor.'

'Maybe,' said Franz, feigning lack of interest. Although secretly he was rather flattered by this assessment — from a public official, no less — of his relationship with the professor. He dabbed the nib of the fountain pen with his little ink sponge, with particular care. 'What exactly is it I'm supposed to have heard?'

'Well, that the professor is leaving. Leaving Berggasse, leaving Vienna, leaving Austria, with family and furnishings, lock, stock and barrel!'

Franz nodded. Something nasty rose up in his throat and stuck there for a moment before rising higher, spreading out somewhere behind his eyes, seeming to fill his entire head. 'Right,' he said, looking down at the columns, his freshly inked entries blurring into a slushy blue mess of numbers.

'Yes, that's how it is,' the postman went on, with an eager nod. 'Because the professor is one of them, too, you know. A

Jew, I mean. And as a Jew on the one hand and a professor on the other, he'll have thought: "I'd rather go before it gets really unpleasant."'

'Aha,' said Franz. 'And where's he planning to go?'

Heribert Pfründner straightened up and shrugged. 'To England, they say. Maybe they'll leave him in peace over there. They have a king, anyway, and plenty of idiots, I expect, who'll pay him something for his ideas.'

'Aha,' repeated Franz. 'And when's he leaving?'

'Tomorrow,' said the postman. The postbag had slipped forward; he slung it onto his back with a circular movement of his torso. 'Tomorrow afternoon at three.'

After the postman had left the shop Franz's head felt as if it were on fire, and it was a while before it had cooled somewhat and was capable of initiating meaningful action. So now the professor was going, too. Everyone was going. It was as if the whole world was upping and going somewhere. Yet he had only just arrived! He put away the accounts book and stationery under the sales counter, went to the back of the shop, splashed cold water on his face, combed his hair with his fingers, went out front again, selected three particularly fine, plump, aromatic specimens from the box of Hoyos, wrapped them in the arts section of the *Bauernbündler*, hid the parcel inside his shirt, locked the shop and set off on the short walk to Berggasse No. 19.

The two plain-clothes policemen were recognizable from

afar. They were sitting close together on the little bench; one had tipped back his head and seemed to be observing the pigeons in the gutters, the other sat leaning slightly forward, staring down at the pavement. It looked as if they had been sitting like that for a very long time, completely motionless, their backsides glued to the bench, but when Franz reached the door and put his finger on the bell for the Professor's practice they were suddenly standing behind him.

'Where are you going?' asked the younger of the two.

'Well — in there,' answered Franz.

'Who to?'

'The professor.'

'What for?'

'I'm bringing him his theatre tickets.'

'What theatre tickets?'

'Burgtheater, of course,' said Franz. 'Middle of the front row of the stalls. Schiller, I think, or Goethe. Something serious, anyway!'

The older man stepped right up to Franz, but he didn't look him in the eyes; instead, he seemed to focus on a point on his forehead or somewhere just above it. 'There's no show for Jews today,' he said. 'Not tomorrow, either. And certainly not the day after. The show's over for Jews. So you can take your theatre tickets and bugger off, and be quick about it. Otherwise I'll stick 'em so far up your arse not even a horse doctor'll find them!'

Franz walked slowly down Berggasse. The policemen had gone back to the bench and resumed their positions: head back looking at the pigeons, head down looking at the pavement. After about fifty metres he turned into Porzellangasse and stopped. The parcel crackled beneath his shirt. He could smell the Hoyos even through the newspaper. Carefully he peeped around the corner. The men were sitting there, unchanged, grey and unmoving as statues. Opposite them, a few steps away from the entrance to the professorial apartment, was a coal merchant's. The wooden doors to the cellar coalhole stood open and the street was covered in coal dust, blackened almost to the middle of the road. Franz was reminded of Anezka's eyelashes. Black, he thought, black as the devil's heart. Loud clattering and the clopping of heavy hooves announced the arrival of a beer cart, approaching from the Danube Canal. The driver clicked his tongue, the horses leaped forward, the cart accelerated and jolted briskly up Berggasse. It was a big cart, laden with eight huge barrels and two apprentices who sat on the back, dangling their legs from the loading bed. As the cart passed between him and the plain-clothes policemen, Franz started running. Bent double, he jogged alongside the shoulder-high wheels, turned sharply as they drew level with the coal merchant's, and in three steps found himself stand-ing before the pitch-black coalhole. He grabbed the frame with both hands, swung himself through, slid down the short coal slide on his bottom, landed on a softly clacking mound of coal, and looked around. Coal was everywhere: shovelled into heaps, packed into sacks, briquettes stacked up in shining black walls, stray lumps scattered all over the ground. Beneath a little window in the back wall stood a grubby desk; in front of it, three sacks of coal were piled on top of each other as a seat. Franz climbed onto the desk, stuck his head out into the open and found himself overlooking a deserted back court-yard. High, grey walls, an old chestnut tree in the middle, here and there an open window, a few crumpled geraniums, the smell of damp whitewash, boiled cabbage and communal toilets. Franz hauled himself up and crawled out. A low door led from the courtyard to the stairwell of number 19. He went up to the first floor, paused for a moment to calm his hammering pulse, then pressed the bell. It was half an age, or precisely forty-seven heartbeats, before the door opened and Anna's narrow face appeared in the crack.

'Good day, I would like to speak to your Herr Papa, if you please,' said Franz.

'My father doesn't see patients any more.' Her voice was high and soft. Her eyes were brown, like the professor's, but a little darker and calmer.

'I'm not here as a patient,' Franz explained, jutting his chin out belligerently, 'but as a close acquaintance, you might say.'

Anna Freud raised her left eyebrow. Franz had always admired people who could perform this feat. In Nussdorf, as far as he could remember, there were only two: Langelmaier, the old teacher in the village school, and his mother. He himself had tried for years, at home in front of the little mirror or bent over the water by the lake, but had never achieved more than a peculiar contortion of the forehead. Anna took off the safety chain and opened the door. She was wearing a rather shabby woollen gown that reached almost to the floor and buttoned up to the neck: a kind of evening coat or housecoat, or dressing gown. Her feet were bare.

'Come with me,' she said, and walked on ahead. They went through the waiting room and a bare outer office and into another room. Anna opened the only piece of furniture, a wardrobe almost as tall as the ceiling, where about twenty pairs of neatly ironed trousers hung side by side. She took one out: earth-coloured, with high turn-ups.

'Put these on.'

Only now did Franz realize how dirty he was. The slide into the cellar had dyed his trousers black, and he was discharging a little cloud of coal dust with every step. Anna turned to face the window, crossed her arms and bowed her head slightly. Franz could see in the reflection that she had closed her eyes. Carefully he slipped out of his trousers and put on hers instead. Women's trousers — a bit too wide in the hips, a bit too tight on the calves, a bit short overall, but they would do. When he was ready she turned and nodded.

Passing through several empty rooms, with only a few crates stacked up here and there against the walls, they arrived outside the professor's consulting room. Anna tapped on the door three times with her fingertips, then opened it gently and, with a brusque inclination of the head, indicated to Franz to enter.

It was several seconds before he spotted the professor. The room had been stripped of all but a few items of furniture and he was lying on a shapeless couch, his head supported by a heap of plump cushions, the rest of his body concealed beneath a heavy woollen blanket. All that remained, apart from the couch, was a huge tiled stove and a glass cabinet full of peculiar figurines, manikins, and grimacing animal faces.

'What are you doing here?' The professor's voice had transformed once and for all into the rasping creak of a rotten branch. He seemed to have lost weight. His head, resting on the cushions, was even more fragile than Franz remembered. His jaw looked as if it had sort of slipped to one side, and it was in constant motion. Franz approached the couch, stepping cautiously across the parquet floor.

'Are you sick, Herr Professor?' he asked, so quietly that he barely heard himself.

'For about forty years,' nodded Freud. 'Only now I spend my time with my hot water bottle on a couch that was actually meant for others. Incidentally, I'd like to offer you a seat, but I'm afraid our armchairs have either been shipped or are already being sat on by some sturdy National Socialist behind.'

'I'm happy to stand, Herr Professor,' said Franz quickly. 'I heard you're leaving?'

'Yes,' Freud grunted, drawing his knees up under the blanket into a sharp triangle.

'Where for?'

'London.' The professor adjusted his glasses on his nose. 'Why are you wearing Anna's trousers?'

'Your daughter was so kind . . . and I . . . I came through the courtyard . . . through the coal cellar . . . because the Gestapo are sitting outside . . .' ·

'The Gestapo . . .' the professor repeated, and it sounded like a stone falling from his mouth.

Just then they were both distracted almost simultaneously, casting their eyes up to where a daddy-long-legs was trembling its way across the ceiling right above the couch. It skittered in a wide arc into a corner, stopped, bobbed back out a little way and was still.

'I brought you something,' said Franz. He took the little parcel out from under his shirt, carefully unwrapped the three cigars from the Arts pages, and offered them to the professor. Freud's face lit up. With unexpected vigour he tossed aside the blanket and sat up. It was only now that Franz realized he was wearing a suit: an immaculate, single-breasted suit of grey flannel, with a waistcoat, starched shirt collar and neatly knotted tie. But no shoes. Freud's feet, small and narrow like a child's, were clad in dark blue socks; the right one had clearly been darned several times around the outer edge of the big toe.

'One for now, one for the journey, one for England, I thought,' said Franz.

Freud contemplated the three cigars, weighing his head gently from side to side. Finally he picked one up with his fingertips and slipped it into his jacket pocket.

'That one is for the United Kingdom,' he said. 'The first puffs in freedom.'

He took the other two cigars, held them up against the light from the window, palpated them gently, inhaled deeply and, on an enthusiastic, rattling breath, squeezed out the words: 'Have you ever held between your teeth something so magnificent, so wonderful, so perfect in its imperfection?'

Franz thought of the vines he and the other boys used to rip out of the undergrowth, cut into finger-lengths with a penknife, and smoke, lying on their backs on the jetty. They tasted vile — woody and bitter — but nobody let it show. Instead, they all lay there pale and quiet, smoking up at the sky, trying to suppress the urge to cough that kept rising in their throats. Sometimes one of them would retreat into the reeds to puke in the water, doubling up among the tall stalks where the silvery char would immediately start fighting over the lumps.

'No, I don't think I ever have, Herr Professor.'

The old man adjusted his jaw in a crooked smile. 'Then it's high time, my young friend!'

At a nod from the professor, Franz hesitantly went over to the glass cabinet and took out a heavy lead crystal ashtray, flanked on either side by a headless terracotta horseman and a small but fairly erect marble phallus. 'I'm not sure, Herr Professor, I've never tried it.'

'Through trying, whole worlds are reinvented,' said Freud cheerfully. 'Besides, I don't want to smoke on my own at our farewell. Sit down!' he added, after taking another rattling breath, and patted the cushion beside him with his left hand.

'On the couch?'

'On the couch.'

Franz sat, carefully. The couch felt surprisingly hard. Hard like the hours the patients had spent on it, he thought, yet not altogether uncomfortable. Whenever the professor moved beside him he felt it immediately; it was like a physical connection.

They smoked the first puffs in silence. The daddy-long-legs on the ceiling had started moving again. It took a few tentative steps out of its corner, then hurried back and seemed to stop once and for all.

On taking his first puff Franz had had to suppress a violent urge to cough; on the second, the urge to throw up; and now, on the third, he felt momentarily faint and had the sense that he was slowly falling forwards onto the parquet. Somehow he managed nonetheless to recover a degree of inner balance, and from then on things began to improve. After about the seventh or eighth puff he could already feel, in addition to the slight paralysis in his tongue, a sense of profound well-being spreading through him, warm as an oven.

'I heard, of course, what happened to Herr Trsnyek,' said the professor, clearing his throat into his small fist. 'I'm very sorry.'

'Yes,' said Franz, after a while. 'Now I'm the tobacconist.'

The room gradually filled with a yellowish twilight. The chestnut tree rustled outside, and dark grey clouds gathered in the little piece of sky above the courtyard. Freud pulled the corner of a blanket over his lap. 'And it's getting cold, as well,' he said grumpily, rubbing his feet together.

'You should put on something warm, Herr Professor. A knitted waistcoat, perhaps. Or a woolly cardigan. Or you could light this tiled stove. And it wouldn't hurt to take a bit more care of your health in general. At your age, I mean!'

The professor feebly waved this away. 'My age left health behind a long time ago.'

'I will not allow you to say such a thing, Herr Professor!' said Franz, raising a stern forefinger.

'Children and old men should be allowed much more than that. But let's talk about a very different complaint. How is your Bohemian Dulcinea?'

'She's not called Dulcinea, she's called Anezka, and it's over. Or rather, it never started. Perhaps the whole thing was a huge mistake, anyway.'

'Love is always a mistake.'

'She's with a Nazi now. An officer. Or general. Or I don't know what. Someone from the SS, anyway, all in black with silver skulls on his belt . . .'

Franz faltered. Suddenly he felt the old man's gaze upon him. They looked at each other for a moment in silence. His eyes, he thought, those strange, brown, bright, shining eyes look as if they're not aging along with the rest of his body. Freud opened his mouth and allowed a little smoke to escape between his teeth; it crept up slowly past his nostrils, behind the lenses of his glasses and over his forehead.

'Back when I boarded the train in Timelkam, my heart hurt,' Franz went on, 'and when Anezka ran away from me the first time, ten doctors wouldn't have been enough to treat the pain. But at least I knew more or less where I was going and what I wanted. Now the pain has almost gone, but I don't know anything any more. I feel like a boat that's lost its rudder in a storm and is now just drifting stupidly here and there.' After a short silence he added: 'In that sense, Herr Professor, you've actually got it much better,' he added, after a short silence. 'You know exactly where you're going.'

Freud sighed. 'Most paths do at least seem vaguely familiar to me. But it's not actually our destiny to know the paths. Our destiny is precisely *not* to know them. We don't come into this world to find answers, but to ask questions. We grope around, as it were, in perpetual darkness, and it's only if we're very lucky that we sometimes see a little flicker of light. And only with a great deal of courage or persistence or stupidity — or, best of all, all three at once — can we make our mark here and there, indicate the way.'

He fell silent, bowed his head, then glanced out of the window. A light rain had begun to fall. The wet leaves of the chestnut tree were shining. Somewhere a door slammed and someone shouted something unintelligible; then all was quiet again.

'That chestnut tree . . .' Freud murmured. 'How many times have I seen it blossom . . .'

'Are there chestnut trees in London, too, Herr Professor?'

'I don't know.' Freud shrugged and looked at Franz. Franz could make out his own reflection in the lenses of Freud's spectacles: a little, thin man with grotesquely distorted limbs. Suddenly a jolt passed through the professor's body; he stuck his cigar between his teeth, pushed himself up from the couch with both hands, managed somehow to straighten up, and stood there for a second, swaying gently. Then he walked over, knees clicking, to the corner of the room, where the daddy-long-legs was crouching high above him.

'Why in the world is he allowed to stay here, when I, the world-famous originator of psychoanalysis, have to go!' he cried. He raised his arm and shook his fist threateningly at the creature. The daddy-long-legs trembled briefly, raised a leg, lowered it again, and stopped moving. Freud glared at it for a while in challenge. Finally he dropped his arm and stared without speaking at the smoke-browned wallpaper.

'I'm sure a daddy-long-legs doesn't always have it easy either, Herr Professor,' said Franz, cautiously breaking the silence. Freud looked at him as if he had just noticed something entirely new, an entirely unknown form of life that, during his long absence, had made itself at home on his couch. He dismissed Franz's comment with a tired wave of his hand. Then he took a puff of his Hoyo, which had already almost gone out, walked back to the couch with small steps, and allowed himself to sink slowly into it as if after immense exertion. It had grown even darker in the room. Outside, thunder was rolling in from a distance and the chestnut seemed to cower in the confines of the courtyard. Inside the house there was almost total silence; only now and then a muffled sound would reach them from one of the rooms further off.

Franz felt the professor's breaths coming and going beside him, sometimes accompanied by a slight clearing of the throat. He could hear the rubbing together of the professorial socks, shortly followed by a series of creaks in the wooden floor, the crackle of the glowing cigar. Then silence again.

'By the way, I didn't buy any of your books in the end,' said Franz. 'Firstly, they're quite expensive, secondly, they're incredibly thick, and thirdly, there's no room in my head for things like that at the moment. I did follow your advice, though, and started writing down my dreams,' he added. 'Most of them are probably nonsense, but there are some funny ones in there. I don't mean laugh-out-loud funny, more sort of funny-peculiar. I don't know where they all come from. Because I can't imagine that such peculiar things could grow in my head all by themselves. Or what do you think, Herr Professor?'

Freud murmured something unintelligible and stretched his legs out in front of him. Franz giggled. 'In any case, I write them on a piece of paper every day and stick them on the shop window. Whether it'll achieve anything remains to be seen. For me personally, I mean. But it's good for the shop. People stop, press their noses against the glass and read whatever's drifted through my mind that night. And as they've already stopped, they sometimes come in and buy something as well.' He paused.

'That's just how it is, Professor!' he continued. He couldn't help giggling again. His whole body was flooded with a warm sense of cosiness. At the same time, he was slightly dizzy. Pleasantly dizzy, though, as if he were sitting not on an old couch but on the far older, rotten jetty on the southern shore of the lake, which was already half sunk in the water and always bobbed so nicely over the waves as they rolled in from the steamer. Maybe it was because of his Hoyo, harvested on the sunny banks of the San Juan y Martínez River and rolled by the tender hands of beautiful women, he thought, and contemplated its delicate, leafy skin for a while. Or the almost unreal proximity of the professor. Perhaps, though (his thoughts ran on) it was because of something quite different, although actually it was completely irrelevant where this warm cosiness had come from all of a sudden — cosy was cosy, and that was that. There was nothing more to think about. Large, solitary raindrops were splashing against the windowpanes, shining streaks driven apart in all directions by the wind. One by one lights went on in the windows on the opposite side of the courtyard.

'You won't know this, Herr Professor,' said Franz, slowly rotating the cigar between his fingers, 'but Otto Trsnyek wasn't a smoker. Otto Trsnyek was a newspaper reader. Newspaper reader and tobacconist. Although for him that was pretty much one and the same. It's funny, really: a man spends decades sitting in his tobacconist's and doesn't want to smoke. He sits there, knows practically everything about cigars, knows their provenance and qualities and distinctive characteristics right down to the last detail and can describe their inner life like a doctor describing the inside of a corpse — but doesn't have even the faintest idea what they actually taste like.' He tapped a long trail of ash into the ashtray positioned between his thigh and the professor's. 'It really is funny,' he repeated thoughtfully. 'Of course, I don't understand much about smoking yet, either. But when you come back I'll know more, I promise. And you will come back. Most definitely, no matter what, you will come back. Because your homeland is your homeland, and home is home. And Hitler'll calm down again one of these days. And all the rest of them, too. And everything will be like before. Or — what do you reckon, Herr Professor?'

Freud made a grumbling noise, and Franz let himself sink a little deeper into the cushions.

'They say that in England it rains more than in the Salzkammergut. So that must be practically all the time. That can't be healthy for a gentleman who's getting on in years, if you'll pardon the expression. In any case, you must meet my mother sometime. I think the two of you would get along well, you see. Because Mama knows a lot about people, too, and all the stupid things they do, so you'd have plenty to talk about. And she can make potato strudel, too. The proper, authentic one: fried in an iron pan with clarified butter, with or without greaves, with or without lentils, however you like it . . .'

Franz fell silent. It seemed to him that he had never talked so much in his life. And perhaps that was true. Previously, not talking had always seemed very desirable to him. What did you need to talk about, really, when you were surrounded by trees, rushes and algae? His mother had never liked to waste words, anyway. Most evenings they would sit together in the cottage in silence, and it was nice like that. Mother. Where was she now? What was she doing? Was she thinking of him at this moment? Of her little Franzl, who was not actually little at all any more? Franz blinked. Outside, rain was pelting against the windows. The cushions at his back were softer than anything he had ever touched in his life. Apart from his mother's arms. And Anezka's

belly. And the hollows at the backs of her knees. And the hill
of her shoulder blade. And the other, quite different parts of
her body. His stomach gurgled quietly. The tiled stove in the
corner answered with a quiet crackle. A shadow floated along
the wall. Something was moving in the display cabinet, too.
A wooden warrior the size of a thumb stood on tiptoe, slowly
raised his hand, and waved as if in farewell. 'That's nonsense,
of course,' said Franz quietly. Or thought out loud. Never in
his life had he felt so tired and heavy.

'Herr Professor?' he asked. His voice trembled slightly;
he held the cigar away from his face and watched as the glowing end went blurry before his eyes. 'You are coming back,
aren't you?'

The professor didn't answer, and when Franz looked at
him he saw that he had fallen asleep. His breathing was regular,
both hands lay quietly in his lap; the stump between his fingers had long since gone out. Franz set down his Hoyo in the
ashtray and bent over the old man. He seemed extraordinarily
delicate. Like the figurines in his display case, thought Franz.
As if, were he to slip off the couch in his sleep and onto the
parquet floor, he might break into a thousand pieces. Or simply turn to dust. His head was tipped back, his mouth slightly
open. His skin looked like yellowed paper that had been crumpled a thousand times and smoothed out again. He lay there,
completely calm; only his eyes were flickering back and forth
beneath his eyelids, as if they didn't want to resign themselves

to the silence and darkness around them. Franz took the cold remnant of the cigar out of the professor's hand and placed it in the ashtray. Carefully he stuffed one of the smaller cushions behind the professor's neck to support it; he straightened the bent shirt collar with his fingertips and gently blew some little flakes of ash off the tie. Then he took the blanket, spread it over the professor's body and stroked his hand over the wool. He stood beside the couch for almost another minute, not moving, watching the professor's quiet breathing. When at last he tiptoed out of the room, he glanced up at the ceiling one more time. The daddy-long-legs had vanished.

The afternoon of the following day — it was the fourth of June, 1938 — Professor Sigmund Freud, along with a sparse group of his closest friends and relatives, left Vienna, the city where he had spent almost eighty years of his life, to take the Orient Express via Paris and on to exile in London. The formalities had been arranged. The exit permits had been issued; the Reich Flight Tax, almost a third of the family fortune, had been paid, and most of the household, furniture and antiquities had either been shipped or was in a warehouse awaiting transportation to England. Why they were nonetheless accompanied by some twenty suitcases, trunks, boxes and bags was a mystery to the professor, as, incidentally, was the fact that the majority allegedly belonged to him. Far too many possessions for an old man, he thought, watching the day pass as if in a dream.

Unnecessary ballast on the final stretch of a long journey. Anna was in charge, and had everything in hand. She ordered the two big taxis to Vienna West Station; she arranged porters, bought the tickets, and gave the official on the counter a few coins to reserve them seats. The passports, visas and other papers of all the travellers in their little group were safely stored in her handbag, and with her in a basket she carried a few slices of cold smoked meat, a pot of her homemade cabbage with noodles and a remarkable quantity of bread dumplings, still warm and wrapped in tea towels. Right at the bottom of the basket she had also hidden a bottle of vermouth and some tiny glasses. For the first few metres after the border, she thought. A toast to freedom. As the little group crossed the arrivals hall, followed by curious glances and a swarm of whispers, Anna's mother burst into tears. Anna passed her a handkerchief and stroked her head, then made it very clear to her that she should pull herself together and keep walking. She had never loved Vienna as her parents did. Or hated it as they did, either. When all was said and done, she had no particular feelings at all for the city of her birth. For her, their departure was nothing more nor less than fleeing from the National Socialists, an act in which they had at last succeeded after all. There was a great throng on the platform. People were shouting, crying and laughing, clasping each other in their arms, kissing or fighting one last time, calling out to one another through the open windows of the train, gathering in little groups, talking loudly all at once, or standing alone beside a suitcase, looking confused, with a pale blue ticket in their hand.

For some reason, Professor Sigmund Freud was absolutely determined to be the last to board. His daughter, however, was pushing him before her with gentle firmness, up the iron steps and into the carriage. 'Leave me alone, I can manage by myself,' he said; and those were his last words on Viennese soil.

Anna surveyed the overcrowded platform once more. The babble of voices seemed to swell beneath the high ceiling of the station hall; the whistle sounded over it, announcing their departure. A late traveller hurried to his carriage; a pair of adolescents fell theatrically into each other's arms; flowers, hats and newspapers were waved; and the red of swastika armbands was all around, flashing amid the confusion. As Anna finally turned away to board the train, something caught her eye. Right at the back, at the entrance to the arrivals hall, where the crowd was at its thickest, stood the young tobacconist. He was standing stock-still with his back to the wall; his face was unusually white, and he seemed to be looking in their direction, but she couldn't see his eyes at this distance. The whistle blew again, the conductor gave the signal for departure, and Anna boarded the train. Once she had closed the door behind her, and the carriage had given a ponderous jolt and started moving, she exhaled deeply and leaned her forehead against the window. The glass was pleasantly cool, and as the train left Vienna West station the afternoon sun shone full in her face.

Things were bearable again. Somehow things can always be borne. At any rate, he seemed to have survived the worst, passed the lowest point, put the most vicious of the stomach pains behind him. Even the hallucinations had almost stopped. Not even a day and a half had passed since Franz had tiptoed across the parquet floor of the Freud family's labyrinthine apartment, searched for the front door, eventually found it, and pulled it to behind him as gently as possible. Even as he was saying farewell by tracing the professor's name with his fingertip on the brass plaque beside the practice bell, his stomach had begun to feel rather peculiar, and by the time he reached the bottom of the stairs this peculiar feeling in his stomach had already become an overwhelming nausea. Reeling like a clumsy puppy he passed through the entrance hall. For a moment he imagined that he was lost in the tunnel of the old salt mine he had visited with his primary school class years earlier on a day trip to Gmunden. Back then he had kept covertly licking the tunnel walls, wanting to taste the salt buried deep in the earth, but each time he did so he was disappointed by the dusty taste of the stone. These memories vanished again as quickly as they had surfaced, and Franz staggered out onto the street. Rain pelted in his face; Berggasse had become a torrent, and a brown soup was bubbling up from under the manhole covers. The bench was empty. But as Franz pushed himself off from the door handle, which he had briefly used to steady himself, and headed for home, he noticed, through the thick veil of rain, a shadowy movement in an archway on the other side of the street. Nothing else happened, though — perhaps it was because of the rain, or perhaps it was because the Gestapo had orders to watch an entrance, not an exit. Either way, Franz was glad of it, and he headed home, doubled over and weaving a bit but otherwise unscathed.

He spent that night and the following morning in bed, with roiling depths beneath him while above, against the backdrop of the tatty ceiling paper, a hazy collection of bizarre figures kissed and rubbed up against each other, limbs entangled, before scattering and evaporating in the stale air of the room. Sometimes his thoughts wandered out into the shop, to the cigars lying quietly in their boxes, some of which were Hoyos de Monterey, and every time they did so he was forced to stick his head in the laundry bucket positioned right beside his bed and allow matters to take their course. Around midday he started to feel a little better, and finally, at half past two in the afternoon, he clambered out of bed on rather wobbly legs and set off on foot for Vienna West Station.

About three quarters of an hour later he was standing on the platform where the crowd was thickest, right at the back of the station hall, watching the professor board the train. The distance was too great for him to be able to see his eyes, but he could see him grinding his jaw as his daughter pushed him up the iron steps. His left hand clutched the grab rail; the right held his hat firmly on his head. At that moment he seemed so slim and light that Franz would not have been surprised if Anna had picked him up in her arms and carried him like a child.

Punctually at 15:25, in accordance with the timetable, the train set off, quickly gathered speed and left the station, heading west. Franz closed his eyes. How many farewells can a person bear, he thought. Perhaps more than we think. Perhaps not even one. Nothing but farewells wherever we stay, wherever we go: we ought to be told this. For a moment he felt the urge just to let himself fall forward and lie there with his face on the platform. A piece of luggage, left behind, lost, forgotten, nothing but curious pigeons pattering round it. That's utter nonsense, he thought angrily. He shook his head and opened his eyes again. He gazed down the tracks one last time as they flashed in the sunshine. Then he turned around and walked back through the arrivals hall and out into the brightness of the Viennese afternoon. The sky was brilliant blue, the rain had washed the asphalt clean, and blackbirds were singing in the bushes. Outside the station entrance was the gas lamp Franz had clung to after his arrival in Vienna. How long ago was that? A year? Half a life? A lifetime? He had to laugh at himself, at the funny boy hanging on to the street lamp here that day, with the resinous smell of the forest in his hair, clumps of mud on his shoes and a few crazy hopes in his head. And suddenly he realised that this boy no longer existed. He was gone. Swept away, perished somewhere in the stream of time. Although it had all happened incredibly fast, he thought; perhaps even a bit too fast, overall. It felt as if he had outgrown himself before his time, or had simply stepped out of his own self, if you could put it like that. All that was left was the memory of a thin shadow underneath a gas lamp. He took a deep breath. The city smelled of summer, horses, diesel and tar. A tram came clanging up the ring road, a little swastika flag fluttering from one of the side windows. He thought of his mother, who perhaps right now was sitting on a jetty warmed by the sun, crying down into the glittering water as it splashed upon the shore. He thought of Otto Trsnyek, his crutches leaning uselessly against the wall in the corner of the shop. And he thought of the professor, who must have left the city boundary far behind him by now and was probably already somewhere over the Lower Austrian potato fields, speeding towards London. Perhaps it was possible to make a mark here or there, to indicate the way, the professor had said. A little flicker of light in the darkness; you couldn't expect more than that. But no less, either, thought Franz, and almost laughed out loud. The tram clanged past and turned into Mariahilferstrasse. The little flag in the window looked as if it were dancing.

'You know, it's a funny thing: the longer the days get, the shorter life feels. It's a contradiction, but that's the way it is. So I ask you: what do people do to make their lives longer and their days shorter? They talk. They talk, chatter, gossip, tell stories, and they do it practically non-stop. And even if you sometimes think you've finally found a bit of peace and quiet — in church, say, or better still, in the graveyard — what do you know: another person starts up, yattering on! It's probably the same up in Heaven, or under the earth: always somebody mouthing off. But I tell you what: most of what comes out of people's faces all day long you can just chuck straight in the bin. Everybody's talking, you see, but nobody knows anything. Nobody knows what they're talking about. Nobody's in the picture. Nobody has a clue. Although these days that's probably better, anyway, not having too much of a clue. Cluelessness is practically the order of the day. Not knowing's the guiding principle. That way you can sometimes look and not have seen anything. Or listen and still not understand. *The truth is the truth and that's that* is what they usually say. But I say that's not how it is! Here, anyway, in our beloved Vienna, there are as many truths as there are windows with people sitting behind them who reckon they've seen or heard or smelled or always knew some thing or another. And what person thinks is the right thing is the biggest piece of foolishness on God's earth to another, and vice versa. Give me a litre of milk, please — or two, actually, always better to stock up! Anyway, the only thing everyone pretty much agrees on is that it must have been last night. Between about three and four. That's the hour of the rats. By then the politicos have finished their shouting, the drunks have found their way home and the milkmen haven't started their rounds yet. Any decent person is in bed at that time of night. Or sitting by the window staring out into the dark. But of course opinions do vary a bit. Some are saying it was more like three, while others are saying it must have been nearly four, because apparently the sky was already turning silver above the roofs. I say, silver my foot! It was pitch dark, there wasn't even a sliver of a moon, the streets were empty, meaning that the scene was all set for the kind of ruffians who like to avoid the light. Although ruffian is relative nowadays. Who can see what goes on inside people's heads? The intentions and inpulses of the human brain are always unfathomable. And a person who yesterday was a ruffian puts on a different hat today and suddenly they're eminently respectable. But don't mind me, I didn't say anything. Give me two hundred grammes of butter and three kilos of potatoes as well, please, but only the little floury ones, for a good dumpling dough. So anyway: it happened between three and four. And there was only one. One person, on his own. A man, of course; because, let's face it, a woman wouldn't waste so much as a second on such a crazy idea. Some say he was most likely middle-aged. Others swear blind that he must have been young because he could run so fast. They say that when it was all over he shot down from

Morzinplatz and up Berggasse like a streak of lightning. A daring lad. But a bit of an idiot, too, if you ask me. When you've got daring, stupidity's never far behind. It was pure luck they didn't catch him straight away — idiot's luck, basically. Well, I mean, think about it: secret police lurking everywhere, on every corner, in front of every shop, in the park, in the restaurants, even in church, everywhere you look there's one of them sitting or standing about — but then they go and forget about their own headquarters! Although actually they didn't completely forget. A couple of them did come running up eventually. But only when it was far too late: morning had broken and the flag had been raised, as it were. Talking of forgetting: do you have a good curd cheese? A Quargel? No, that one's no good, it doesn't smell. Quargel has to smell or it isn't Quargel. Put it back, add a couple of beers and make up the bill for me, please. So as I was saying — pitch black, no stars, no moon, and no streak of silver above the city. Which is why, when all's said and done, none of the curtain-twitchers can know exactly what happened. People only keep watch out of spite. But because spite is inquisitive on the one hand and blinds you on the other, people only see what they want to see! Anyway, what's indisputable is that he was able to get at one of the three big flagpoles right in front of the Hotel Metropol unbothered by either the Gestapo or his own conscience. You know the ones: the three big swastika banners that cast a shadow over half the square and always rattle so insistently in the wind. He set about

working on the middle one. Simply cut the cord, pulled the
pretty swastika down from its lofty height and let it fall on the
dusty ground. They found it later, lying there all runkled up
and dirty. Shame about the pretty fabric. Then he apparently
pulled out a parcel from under his shirt. Others are saying,
though, that there was no such parcel and he was carrying the
corpus delicti around with him just like that, not wrapped up at
all. If you ask me, details like these make no difference in the
end. All that counts are the facts, which are: he cut the cord,
he threw the Hitler cross in the dirt, and he fastened that
thing — whether taken from a parcel or not — in its place, ran
it up and hoisted it like the holy flag of Jerusalem. Then he was
gone. Like lightning. They say he saluted up at the night sky
but I reckon that's a rumour, or sheer exaggeration, just some
of the curtain-twitchers bragging. In any case, the sun was well
up by the time the Gestapo came running, meaning half of
Vienna had already had a chance to spread mischievous gossip.
So now, of course, imagine the agents' faces! What an unbelievable blunder! Because hanging there on the middle flagpole,
right at the top, with the first rays of the morning sun upon it,
was a pair of trousers. A pair of brown men's trousers with a
pleated waistband, as far as you could see from the ground.
They just hung there: a bit crumpled, a bit baggy, but otherwise immaculate; nondescript, really. But as is well known, it's
often precisely the nondescript that hides something truly scan-
dalous. Which is why there was immediately a tremendous fuss

on the ground. Everyone was arguing with everyone else, all shouting at one another, and what with all the excitement it was quite a while before anyone thought of getting the trousers down. Then, just when it finally occurred to someone to pull on the cord, something quite remarkable happened. Because at that moment the wind picked up. A sudden gust of wind, a flurry, a breeze, whatever you want to call it. Anyway, all of a sudden this wind started blowing, and it caught in the trousers and sort of lifted them up. And now of course you can really imagine those secret service faces twisting into a whole range of expressions of stupid astonishment or astonished stupidity. Because it wasn't a normal pair of trousers. It was basically only half a one. A one-legged trouser, it was. The other trouser leg was sewn up at about knee height. So the wind blew into this pair of one-legged trousers just as they were trying to get it down. And then right in front of everyone's eyes something truly strange happened. For a while the trousers just flapped about a bit but then all of a sudden they stood still, they basically lay horizontal in the air. And just for a moment this brown, crumpled, rather baggy trouser leg up there in the sky looked like a pointing finger. Like an enormous pointing finger, showing people the way. Where exactly it was pointing, of course, is speculation at best. Away, I reckon, at any rate: far, far away. So — now would you be so kind and give me a bar of chocolate, too. With nuts. And I'd like to pay next time, if there's no rush. Thank you very much indeed, have a good day, goodbye!'

All night Frau Huchel had lain awake staring up into the deep darkness between the roof beams. In the course of the previous evening she had increasingly felt a strange unease, a malaise, like a mild fever. Perhaps it's the womanly flushes already, she thought. Perhaps I'm at that stage now. She had gone to bed early, but sleep refused to come, so she lay there staring up into the dark and listening out into the silence. The silence in a fisherman's cottage, she thought, sounded different from the silence in the forest, for example. Or the winter silence below the summit of the Schafberg. Or the silence a person sometimes carried in her heart. The thing with the good-looking tourist guide had soon turned out to be a mistake, just a short-lived fantasy, and a few days ago the innkeeper had made a pass at her again. He had put his hand on the back of her neck in the restaurant kitchen and asked for more. This time, too, she had threatened him with the fictional Obersturmbannführer Graleitner, but the innkeeper had remained unimpressed. Why had this Herr Graleitner never shown his face around here, he had asked, slowly sliding his hand down her back. Instead of answering, she had taken the large bone cleaver out of the drawer and, with a single calm incision, slit open the front of his apron. The innkeeper had stood there, suddenly paralyzed, as the apron fell open like a grubby curtain, exposing his broad loins. Afterwards she had rammed the knife into the wooden worktop and walked out. So now she was unemployed, but not that unhappy about it. The air was hot, her body was hot, and the hours stole through the cottage like listless shadows. When the moon appeared in the flue vent above the stove, filling the room with its pallid light, she placed her right hand over her heart and wept. For a few minutes she felt at peace, but then the unease spread inside her again and banished the last of the tears. Outside a bird flapped out of the reeds, beat its wings hard against the water and laughed like a hoarse child. She could make out the first light of dawn in the little window facing the lake. She rose and went outside. Barefoot, she walked down to the lake. The grass was damp and cool. Grey streaks of mist drifted across the surface of the water, and behind them, just visible, were the contours of the opposite bank. She stood there like that for a long time, letting the water lap around her feet and watching the lake slowly fill with light. A shoal of young char flitted about her ankles, cormorants sailed past high above her head, and a little way off the three big swastikas materialized out of the mist. Franz's mother heard her heart beating. A little shudder ran down her back, and she shivered, although it was warm. 'My boy,' she said, closing her eyes. 'Where are you, my boy?'

When Franz awoke, he laughed. It was just an abrupt sound thrown at the ceiling of his room, but it seemed to him as if, up there, this laugh burst open, streaming across the old wallpaper in all directions. He blinked and rubbed his eyes. The night had been a short one. Almost too short to dream. A few scraps of dreams had wandered in nonetheless, and were now still shimmering faintly somewhere deep inside him. Quickly he picked up pencil and paper and scribbled down a few words. He got out of bed, dressed, and went out onto the street with the paper and a roll of sticky tape. A radiant new day had dawned; Währingerstrasse lay bathed in the soft brightness of the morning sun, and the first passers-by were heading for the centre of town, chasing long shadows before them. Franz stood on tiptoe, stretched his arms up in the air and yawned. As always, he had woken precisely at shop-opening time. A real tobacconist doesn't need an alarm clock, Otto Trsnyek had once said, and he was right. Franz set about sticking the paper onto the shop window. A new dream, a new day, he thought, and the panes could do with a wash again. Behind him he heard the burble of a diesel engine, getting louder. A dark, old-fashioned car approached from the direction of the Votive Church and stopped directly in front of the tobacconist's. Three men got out, among them the official with the mournful face.

'We've already had the pleasure,' he said. 'Shall we introduce ourselves anyway?'

Franz shook his head. The mournful man took a cigarette case out of his coat pocket, extracted a thin cigarillo, lit it, and observed Franz as he tore off strips of sticky tape with his teeth and carefully stuck the paper on the window. A metallic crackling sound came from the engine compartment of the car.

'Well,' said one of the men sadly, running his hand over the bonnet. 'Time's getting on.'

The mournful man gave him a dirty look and he fell silent. Behind him a woman bumped over the cobbles on a heavy bicycle, whistling softly through her teeth with every tread on the pedals. A window opened on the other side of the street; a hand appeared holding a pair of scissors, and cut off the head of a geranium. It plopped onto the window ledge, fell onto the pavement and lay there, glowing brightly. The mournful man sighed, dropped his cigarillo on the ground and trod it out.

'Why do the days have to be so long now, even at the crack of dawn,' he said, with a tired shake of his head. 'Shall we?'

'Just a moment,' said Franz. He bent a little closer to the paper and, concentrating hard, stuck another strip over it.

'There's no point to that any more, sonny boy,' said the mournful man.

'What has a point and what doesn't remains to be seen,' said Franz. 'Also, my name is Franz. Franz Huchel from Nussdorf am Attersee!'

'You can be Franz from the Tyrolean mountains as far as I'm concerned,' said the mournful man amicably, 'or Hans from Unterfladnitz, or anyone from anywhere. We don't make distinctions. All our guests are treated equally at the Hotel Metropol. So shall we go, or do I have to get cranky first?'

Franz tore two last strips from the roll and stuck them diagonally across the whole piece of paper. He placed his hand flat upon it and closed his eyes. The paper felt warm, and it was as if the window underneath were breathing, a scarcely discernible rising and falling beneath his palm. When he opened his eyes again, he saw that his fingers were trembling.

'I have to lock up,' he said. 'Because who knows what will happen.' He closed the door and turned the key three times. As he walked between the men to the car, he thought he could still hear the little bells tinkling quietly behind him. But that's nonsense, he thought, and got in.

Almost seven years later, on the morning of the twelfth of March 1945, a strange silence lay over the city. The night had dissipated like smoke, giving way to a murky half-light. Thunderstorms were forecast on the radio, and the wind was whipping up dust in the streets and blowing loose sheets of newspaper before it. In the past few days there had been more rumours of fresh bombing raids; everyone was talking about it, but no one knew any details. Anyone who didn't absolutely have to go out on the street stayed at home or spent their time in bunkers and cellars. At night, here and there in the unlit streets, there were glimmers behind cellar windows, and if you bent down and looked through the murky glass you would see the flickering faces of people sitting around a few candles, silently playing cards. Währingerstrasse was almost empty. An old woman sat on a bench scattering crumbs among the pigeons that pattered excitedly at her feet. Pigeons were the only birds still to be seen in the parks and on the streets. All the others had vanished the previous autumn. Early one morning, as if responding to a secret call, they had gathered together in great flocks and left the city, heading west. The old lady let out a cry of alarm as one of the creatures almost fluttered into her lap. She slipped the little bag with the remaining crumbs into the pocket of her coat, heaved herself to her feet and, grumbling quietly, limped inside the nearest building.

A young woman approached from the ring road, walking quickly. Her head was lowered, and she had buried her hands deep in the pockets of a man's jacket that was far too big for her; it hung like a sack from her shoulders and reached to below her knees. As she opened her mouth in a hiss to scare away the pigeons fighting over the last remnants of food, her teeth were momentarily visible: small and shimmering white, like pearls, with an unusually large gap right in the middle.

Anezka crossed the road and stopped. A coal cart was coming towards her. The two Haflinger horses in front were puffing their steamy breath ahead of them, and the coalman was perched on the box. His eyes were dull and tired, two pale flecks in his black face as he gazed out over the horses' heads. The cart drove past, noisy and clattering, and Anezka followed it with her eyes until it turned into Boltzmanngasse and disappeared. She walked past Veithammer Installations and a few steps later stood in front of the former Trsnyek's Tobacconist's. The paint was peeling off the doorframe, and the shop window was coated in a fine layer of dust. Anezka leaned her forehead against the glass and peered inside. The shop was empty apart from the old counter, the shelves along the walls, and the stool, which lay in the middle of the room like a dead animal with its legs pointing upwards. The door at the back was ajar; the room beyond it was dark. Anezka put her hands and cheek against the pane and closed her eyes. For a brief moment she had the feeling that the window, the room, the ground, the air were vibrating. She breathed on the glass and slowly, with her forefinger, drew two lines where it clouded over. As she turned to go, she saw the piece of paper beside the door. It was really just a scrap, yellowed by the sun and almost black around the edges. The bottom half was missing; it had been ripped off or had simply fallen away with the years. The rest had only survived because it was criss-crossed and covered with several strips of tape. Anezka recognized the writing without ever having seen it before. It was faded and barely legible beneath the layer of dust; the letters were small and wobbly, almost as if a child had scribbled them. She leaned in close and read:

June 7, 1938
The lake has seen better days, too, the geraniums glow in the night, but it's a fire, and anyway there will always be dancing; the light dis

The rip in the paper went right through the last word. Anezka took a deep breath; then she cautiously peeled off the sticky tape, folded the paper and put it in the pocket of her coat. She looked inside the tobacconist's once more, but there was nothing there. She tapped her finger gently on the window and walked off. As she passed the former Rosshuber butcher's she again had the sense that the air around her was vibrating. This time, though, it was no illusion, and by the time she reached the Votive Church and started to quicken her step, then finally to run as fast as she could, the sky was already filled with the rapidly swelling sound of the Allied bombers' engines as they approached from the west like a huge, dark swarm, casting the city into shadow.